ALWAYS BEEN WRITE

JAMI ROGERS

To Christian ...
I'm so happy for you that he wasn't just a friend.

❀ Formatted with Vellum

ALWAYS BEEN WRITE

JAMI ROGERS

PROLOGUE
TOBIAS

**Author Note: This scene was included in part of the epilogue from More Than Write. **

The Night They Met - (ten or so years ago)

"Happy birthday to one of the best guys I know, Tobias, and congratulations on your first book deal, Zane!" Beck cheers loudly before he, Zane, Simon, Hero, Graham, and I clink our shot glasses together.

The Fireball burns all the way down.

One by one, my friends slap me on the shoulder, and I fist-bump Zane before wandering back into the living room where the majority of the party is taking place.

About a year ago, the six of us met in a creative writing class, where we discovered we're all male romance writers. We've been a tight group from day one. I've had people in the past who were supportive of my dream to write, but nothing compares to having good friends who share the same goals as you. They just get it.

A month ago, I rented an off-campus house. Beck, Simon, and Hero live here with me, while Graham and Zane have their own apartments.

This is the first party I've had here since we moved in. It's June. It's my birthday month, and tonight has been so great that I'm considering making this an annual tradition. Not just for my birthday but also because the guys and I have such busy schedules during the school year. Somehow, we manage to cram writing time into our days, but to hang out, have some beers, and enjoy ourselves, those are rare times.

As I said, we all have big goals. Bestsellers, six-figure contracts, awards, movie deals, serial show deals, audio deals, billboard signs, and so much more.

Determination and dedication aren't something we lack.

I lean against the doorway between the kitchen and the living room. I don't know half the people here. The turnout looks like word spread. Living in a college town can do that. But I don't mind it.

I'm glad I could host a fun night like this for everyone.

"Dude, look," Hero says, coming up behind me as he cracks open a new beer. "Who is that?"

He nods to the front door, where a group of girls just walked in.

"Which one?" I ask, my gaze instantly falling on the last one to step through the door. She's taller than the others, but not by much. Maybe five ten, five eleven. She's got on a pair of cut-off shorts, slip-on sneakers, and a pink one-shoulder top that really brings out the color of her tan skin. She has straight, shiny brown hair pulled into a high ponytail. It's so dark that it might actually be black. I'd need to get closer to know. Her big brown doe eyes scan the room as she takes a breath. My guess is she doesn't know anyone here. I should be a good host and introduce myself while offering her and her friends a drink.

"The one in the blue dress," Hero says.

I smile.

I have no clue who either of them is. I'm just glad he wasn't checking out the same woman as me.

"No clue. But this is our house, so let's go over there."

Hero is one step ahead of me, but I hear a crash in the kitchen behind us. Some guy just dropped a whole tray of shot glasses. I sigh, letting my buddy take over greeting our new guests.

"This is why we set out the paper cups," I say, pointing to the stacks of cups.

"Sorry, we just wanted actual shot glasses."

"Clearly," I say and clean up the mess.

I'd make him do it, but his stumble on the way to the patio says he'd probably worsen the problem.

I glance at the clock. It's only nine, and people are already this drunk.

Hell.

I grab the four bottles of hard liquor sitting out and jog them up the stairs to my room. I don't mind sharing, but beer will be just fine for everyone here on out until the night is over. Maybe it'll slow some of these people down.

As I descend the stairs, I glance at the door. The girl in the pink shirt isn't anywhere in sight. But I do spot Hero chatting it up with the girl in the blue dress.

Simon and Beck are playing video games on the couch,

and Graham is trying to read a book while the redhead next to him is basically trying to climb into his lap. I make my way through the kitchen, grab a fresh beer, and head out to the patio where Zane is chugging a red cup at one end of the beer pong table.

It almost feels like we're at a frat party. I'm sure we would be if it were fall and the semester had started. But tonight, we're basically just a bunch of college kids who either live here full-time or stay to take classes over the summer.

I chuckle to myself.

Does this mean my house is full of like-minded people who know what they want in life and are eager to get there, or is it full of nerds who like summer school?

"Is something funny?"

With a smirk still on my lips, I turn my gaze to the woman next to me, only to come face-to-face with pink shirt girl.

My smile widens.

"Hi," I say instead of answering her question.

Under the patio lights, I can faintly spot the light pink color in her cheeks.

"Hi," she replies.

Before I can say anything else, a Ping-Pong ball smacks her in the temple. She's not injured for obvious reasons, but it does startle her enough to drop her drink.

Her beer spills onto the ground between us.

"Sorry!" Zane yells. "But I get a free pass tonight!"

I grab the ball and toss it back hard enough that it pegs him in the forehead.

Pink shirt girl laughs.

"Sorry, my friends are kind of crazy," I say. "That one just got his first book deal, and he's going insane right now to celebrate."

She smiles wide. "You hang out with people who write books?"

"Don't sound so surprised."

"It's just weird, is all. I mean, college guys barely read, and here you are with someone who writes actual books."

Her tone is flirty, and her smile hits me right in the heart.

I fucking like that smile.

"Oh, stereotyping, are we?" I flirt back, crossing my arms and widening my stance as I wait for her reply.

She shakes her head.

"Nope. Just speaking from experience to all the college guys I've met so far."

I chuckle, wink at her, and then lean closer. "Want me to blow your mind?"

She laughs, and my heart swells.

I've never heard a laugh that physically gives me energy. I want to listen to it again.

"Is that a sex joke I don't get?"

"No." I step even closer to her.

I swear she leans in, too.

"Actually," I say in a whisper, "I write too."

"No, you don't. You're just trying to impress me after the comment I just made."

"It's the truth. Me and my friends. There are six of us. We all write romance."

Her smile twitches, as if she is unsure whether to smile, laugh, or just walk away because I'm now that weird guy.

"Prove it," she says, and honestly, that wasn't what I was expecting her to say. "Let me read something you wrote."

"Seriously?"

"Yeah"—she bumps my shoulder— "or I'll think it's just a line you give to get into a girl's pants."

"All right." I hold out my hand. "Follow me."

"Where to?"

"My room."

"Oh no, I set myself up for that one, didn't I?" But she follows me.

"I'll be a true gentleman," I tell her. "Unless you tell me to be different."

"What a gentlemanly thing to say."

I tug her behind me through the kitchen and up the stairs. Just as we reach my door, I turn to face her.

"By the way, I'm Tobias. What's your name?"

She blushes as I open the door.

"Natalie."

CHAPTER ONE
TOBIAS

Present Day

A bad day can always be fixed by writing. It doesn't even have to be a lot of words. Maybe just a couple hundred. And it doesn't have to be in one of the many romances I'm currently writing. I could just open a blank document and write precisely what I'm thinking, get it off my mind. Of course, I could just share my thoughts with my friends—I trust them more than anyone else—but writing has never let me down either. Both are a solid choice.

I glance up from my computer. All my friends are here with me today. No matter where our lives take us, we always make time once a week to get together and write. We dabble in all areas of the romance genre, but writing is what brought us together. Maybe that's why I trust it so much. It's brought a lot of good into my life. Words are powerful and change lives more than most people realize.

Today is a quiet day at The Space. The Space is a public

workspace Simon, one of the guys sitting at this table, and I opened last year. We both had our reasons for wanting to open this place, but we share this: no matter how much our lives changed over the years, we wanted the group to always have a place to get together.

Sure, we could have picked someone's home, but we're realistic. Aside from me, they're all on their way to getting engaged, married, or growing their families, and having a group of six adult men show up to take over the living room or kitchen to work doesn't seem sensible.

"Something on your mind?" Hero asks, sitting across from me.

I shake my head. "Just thinking about this scene."

And how to finish it, because who are these characters? I have no idea anymore.

I glance at the word count. Thirty thousand words later, and what the hell have I been writing?

Typical.

"Do you want to talk about it?" Zane, who is sitting next to Hero, asks as he looks up.

One by one, Graham, Beck, and Simon also move their attention from their laptops to me. This is an open opportunity, but I take a quick glance at the time. They'll all be heading out soon. I'm not sure what my problem is when it comes to writing these days, so I don't even know where to begin.

"No. I think I've got it," I lie. "I'm just trying to figure out how to rephrase the opening paragraph."

They all nod as if they get it, and I'm sure they do in a way. Writing is a challenging career. We second-guess ourselves almost daily, but god, I love it. In addition to making a story come full circle, the thrill of problem-solving a plot and seeing the characters reach the happily ever after they deserve—I can't get enough of it.

Still, something is off with me. I haven't finished a book in two years. *Two years.*

I write about 75 percent of the story and then I stop. I move on to a new one. Over and over. I have nine unfinished books saved on my computer. I know sticking to my niche and sticking to my style is what my readers want, but I'm … uninspired, maybe. I don't know.

I rub the back of my neck and let out a breath.

Fuck. What is wrong with me?

The entrance door opens, pulling Hero's attention. "It's crazy how busy this place gets. It's no wonder you opened a second location in Colorado."

"We're looking at properties to expand to a third location, also in Colorado," I tell them. Turns out, people really love having a place they can go. Since we don't sell food or drinks, people can bring in anything they like, and honestly, I'm not shocked that the residents of Wind Valley take care of this place as if it were their own. I had been worried it would get trashed by the occasional lazy person, but so far, so good.

Our low membership fees are also why this place has been so busy. People have the Internet at home, so we had to ensure it would be worth it. Location is also a plus. Somewhere to go instead of driving home when they're already downtown. Wind Valley isn't a big city, but it could still take some fifteen to twenty minutes to get across town.

Not to mention that over this past summer, we dove head-first into making this space available for weddings, parties, work meetings, or whatever someone needs.

It's been more successful than we imagined. When we started, I thought it would take up a lot of writing time, but it doesn't. So I know starting and running this company with Simon isn't my problem.

I built a place for me to write.

I just can't seem to do it.

"Really? A third location?" Beck asks with surprise in his eyes. "That's amazing."

He pats Simon on the back and then reaches across the table to give me knuckles.

I chuckle. I've known these guys for twelve years now, and sometimes I feel like we forget how old we are.

Do guys in their thirties still give knuckles?

Obviously, the answer is yes since I just did it.

"Lucky for us," Simon speaks up, "Tobias is willing to take on more work here in the scheduling department, and he's done most of the traveling. He's basically running it on his own."

I laugh and shake my head. "Once we sign that new lease, it's just scheduling and then crossing our fingers that contractors and designers do their job by the time they say they will. Plus, we're in different places in life. The work here is equal as far as I see it."

Beck clears his throat, and when silence falls over the table, I know they're all itching to make a follow-up comment. The part about where we are in life.

No one speaks up, and for that, I'm grateful.

My dating life, or lack thereof, has been a hot topic lately. I've lost count of the number of times they have all mentioned someone they think I should ask out: the new barista at Loves a Brewing, the woman who moved in next door to Hero and

Nora, the woman who just ran by the window and looks like she might be single. Yes, that happened last week.

I get it. They're in love and want that for everyone around them. I'm not even mad that they want me to have what they have. It's just not in the cards for me right now.

I need to figure out this writing rut I'm in first.

Sighing, Zane looks at his watch. "I need to get going. Willa and I have been trying out new recipes for the blog she and Greer started, and she needs me to stop at the store."

"That reminds me," Simon says as he closes his computer. "I have a bag of stuff in my car that Greer says is important for the photo aesthetics on their new page."

One of my favorite things about my friends is, not only are we all driven people but the people who have become part of our lives are too. Every single one of them is out there making their dreams come true, and they've managed to find the perfect partner to stand behind them on the way.

I'll admit I'm a bit of a sappy guy regarding my friends, but hell, I got lucky. I'm not afraid to admit it.

Slowly, Graham, Hero, and Beck pack their things too.

"Dinner at my house next weekend," Hero calls out.

"Next weekend?" Becks clarifies.

"Yeah."

"Natalie's engagement party is next weekend."

"Oh, right. I forgot."

All eyes drift to me.

Again.

"What now?" I ask, not moving from my spot. I intend to finish more work before heading home for the day.

"Nothing," Hero says while Beck and Graham mumble something I imagine is along the same lines.

For as long as I can remember, all my friends have had this fantasy that my best friend Natalie Miller and I are supposed to end up together.

No matter how many times we both tell them that we are nothing more than friends, just friends, the best of friends, actually, it's like they don't hear us. Hell, Natalie is getting married, and as Beck just mentioned, her engagement party is next weekend. An engagement and a wedding all in under six months seems fast to me, but maybe that's just how it goes for some people.

Truth be told, I think that's more a Griffin, her fiancé, thing than a Natalie thing. I've known her for a decade and rushing seems way more like her fiancé's style. Then again, he did take four years to propose to her, so what do I know?

I wave goodbye as the guys all leave me behind. I glance around The Space—our members are all focused on their work. My group had been sitting at the biggest table in the room, and now that the guys are gone, there's no sense in me taking up space out here.

I grab my things and head into the office in the back.

Maybe it's time I did something significant with my life: move to a different state or perhaps even date someone and actually put effort into it.

Neither of those thoughts appeals to me, though.

I love Wind Valley and want to stay here. If I ever left, it would be to Lovers, where my grandma lives, but I don't see that happening anytime soon.

I close the door behind me, and as soon as I pull out the chair and sit down, a text comes in.

NATALIE

Hey, Casanova! Are we still on for
tomorrow?

I groan at her nickname for me. Ten years. Ten years, and she
won't give me a new one. I think I've earned it by now. Then
again, I've only ever had one for her, but since she met Griffin, it doesn't feel suitable to use it. I just call her Natalie or
Nat now, and she seems okay with it.

TOBIAS

Pizza at my place, and let's pick a new
nickname for me.

NATALIE:

Perfect. I'll bring my laptop so we can go
over your social media posts for next
month. And not a chance 🙂

Splendid. That's exactly what I want to do right now when my
writing career is at a standstill: create social media posts. But
hell, just because I'm stuck on the words doesn't mean I need
to fail in all areas.

TOBIAS

Bring your A-game for the posts.

NATALIE:

Oh no. What happened?

TOBIAS:

Do you want the extended version or the short one?

NATALIE:

Short for now. Long later.

TOBIAS:

The short version is that I still haven't written a book for my editor, so she removed me from her list.

NATALIE:

Do you want me to come by now? I have time. We can talk it out. You know what? Don't answer that. I'm headed your way.

Typical Natalie. Outside of the guys, she's the one person who has always been there for me. She supports me in ways I never imagined a friend could. Hell, she was the first person I told I wrote romance, outside of the guys and my grandma Betty. She knew before my parents and my little sister, Quinn.

I knew the moment I met Natalie that she would be different, but this moment reminds me just how lucky I am to have her in my life.

Hell, she's supposed to be planning a wedding, but she's ready to drop everything to help me instead.

Yeah, she and Nora own the company that does all my social media and promotions, but Natalie was doing it way before they started getting paid for it.

TOBIAS:

I'll be fine till tomorrow. I have other things
to keep me busy.

NATALIE:

Are you sure? I can be there in five minutes.

TOBIAS:

I'm sure. See you tomorrow night.

NATALIE:

I'm bringing the newest book from Dana
Volney for you to binge-read. Maybe you
just need to escape.

TOBIAS:

I always like a good escape. It's the best
palate cleanser.

NATALIE:

If you change your mind, let me know.
Griffin left this morning for San Francisco,
so I'm free.

I'm about to text her back when my computer dings. It's like a
sign that I need to get off my phone and get back to work.

So I settle into my seat and open the computer.

First up is an email from my agent, Doug.

Good ole Doug has been with me and all the guys since
college. He didn't go to school planning to be a literary agent,
but he met us, and things kind of snowballed for him. Now
he's running the most well-known agency in the industry and
producing bestsellers, movies, and television shows daily. Of
course, none of those are my books because I currently suck
at writing. Specifically, completing a story.

Maybe this is how I go out, you know? How my career ends.

Doug's email will be something I need to process, so I choose to get it out of the way. If I don't read it, I'll obsess over it, and then I really won't get any work done.

About a month ago, I caved and finally told Doug I was struggling to finish a book. Before that, I just gave him the line "I'm working on it" or "I'm almost done" or my personal favorite, "I just need one more round of edits." Admitting failure isn't easy for me. Doug recommended that I send him the first few chapters of each title, and he would shop around at different publishing houses. I'd love to self-publish them like most of my backlist, but maybe if someone else saw their potential, I'd finish one. I don't know. At this point, I'm so desperate to finish a book that I will try anything. What I do know is, according to Doug, my name is well known enough that some publishers would contract me even on an incomplete, but today is not that day.

I read quickly, but the words *boring, slow, weird, cliché*, and *out of character* all stand out like bold letters.

Well, if I wasn't feeling like my career was stalled before, I sure am now.

CHAPTER TWO
NATALIE

"Did you ask him?"

I sigh and then balance the phone between my shoulder and ear while I pack my work bag. I'm heading over to Tobias's house for a pizza and work dinner tonight. It's how we have planned his social media posts since we met. I might own a company with my other best friend Nora, but that doesn't mean this Tobias and Natalie tradition has to change.

"No. I was going to, but he brought up a work thing, and I didn't think it was the right time."

I can practically hear Nora rolling her eyes at me.

"You know he's not going to be happy about it," she says. "Griffin's sister can be a lot to handle."

"Trust me. I know."

I know you're supposed to love the family you're marrying into, but Griffin's family is different. To sum it up, I think my fiancé, Griffin, was adopted. His father doesn't care for me, and I have no idea why. I've never done something to offend him. I'm not poor and don't come from a broken family—his father has voiced that he's not a fan of *those* people. My family is from Wyoming. My parents are still married, and as far as I know, they never struggled to pay their bills. We are just your average Joe, happy, loving family. Then we have Griffin's mother, who somehow just can't remember my name. I've settled with just letting her call me Nikki at this point. Griffin swears he's never even dated a girl named Nikki, so who knows where she got it, and his sister is … wild. That's all I'm going to say about that.

Then you have sweet, charming, considerate, and thoughtful Griffin, who makes me smile every single day.

So yeah, adoption has to be the answer.

"He's not going to be impressed that you waited until the last minute."

"True, but in my defense, I didn't think Griffin would want him there."

We're driving to Lovers this weekend, a small town just a couple of hours away, to look at Lovers Lodge. It's where the ceremony and reception will take place. It was Griffin's mother's choice, but I didn't argue because it is pretty. I thought it would just be me and Griffin going, but his sister is coming with us now. I wanted to invite my family, but my parents are babysitting while my older sister and brother-in-law are out of town. Nora has her hands full with her own baby, so that leaves Tobias, and I wasn't about to start that never-ending fight with Griffin. But a couple of days ago, Griffin mentioned over the phone that he was happy with the idea of me inviting Tobias to join us.

I've been meaning to ask him to come ever since.

But like Nora said, Griffin's sister, Cassie, can be a lot.

A. Lot.

"I'll ask him tonight when I see him. I'm packing up to go over there now."

"Good. You need someone in your corner when you get to the lodge. Tobias is the perfect choice."

Yeah, let's just hope that he says he'll do it. I know it was just a text, but it sounded like he had a lot on his mind with work.

"I'll let you know what he says," I tell her. "Talk to you tomorrow."

"Sounds good. Bye."

I hang up and drop my phone into my purse to finish packing. When I'm all set, I grab said phone and take a selfie, sending it to Tobias.

NATALIE

A-game ready.

He snaps a selfie back, holding up two Ben and Jerry pints in front of his smiling face.

TOBIAS:

Hurry up.

I'm out the door in the next instant.

* * *

I love having a job where I can make my hours and work from anywhere. Days like today make me love it even more.

I walk into Tobias's house as if it were my own and plop my things onto the kitchen table.

I hear him jog down the steps and come to a stop as he rounds the corner to the kitchen. He shakes his head and leans his hip against the counter.

He studies me with a scowly smile—it's a thing with him. I smile back despite his facial expression. I know Tobias better than he thinks, and even though he's looking at me like I've just disturbed him, he's in a good mood.

"If you keep looking at me like that, you'll get a funny wrinkle in the spot between your eyes." I move around the table and try to reach over the counter to press my finger to that spot on his face, but he swats my hand away.

"So?"

"So, you're too young for wrinkles."

"Maybe I want the wrinkles. Some women love the older man look."

I let out a bubbling laugh.

"Sure. Maybe the young ones. Are you planning to start robbing the cradle, Casanova?"

He groans. "Don't call me that."

"Okay, Casanova."

"Seriously, Nat. It's been years."

"That doesn't change the fact that the night we met, I was convinced you were pulling the ultimate line on me. Or lines. Like a whole scheme."

The sound of his laugh warms me. His laugh is like home; I've missed it for the past few weeks.

I've been busy with wedding plans and preparing for the party next weekend. It turns out that picking out the right place settings and making a list of your friends and family is a lot harder than it sounds. It doesn't help that Griffin and I have the opposite taste in many things. Ergo, we can't pick a spot for a honeymoon. He wants sightseeing, checklists, and plans. I want sun and relaxation and to spend time together without being required to be somewhere.

It wasn't that his ideas were terrible. In fact, they're places I hope to see one day, but not for a honeymoon. Griffin wasn't getting it, and we were getting frustrated. We ended that specific call just minutes ago. I got out of my car, grabbed my things, and headed into the one place I knew put me at peace: Tobias's house.

I still can't believe I'm having an engagement party. I didn't think I'd be the kind of girl to go all out. I'm not, but Griffin wanted to do all the wedding-related planning, and I didn't have any reason to tell him no. He wants us to celebrate as much as we can. What kind of girl would argue with that? I just do what he asks at this point.

"Well, you were in for quite the surprise the night we met, weren't you?" Tobias moves around the counter, watching me as he takes a seat at the table.

"More than I ever thought possible. Did you already order the pizza?" I ask.

"It's four o'clock."

I shrug. "We used to eat dinner this early all the time."

"Yeah, and then party and eat a second dinner at ten or eleven. My body can't do that anymore."

I nod. "Is that what the eight-pack staring back at me says?"

He glances down at his body quickly, then smirks.

"Okay, so maybe there are still a lot of things I can do with this body."

I roll my eyes.

"Okay, let's not get a big head or any—don't even start!" I point a finger at him as I process what I said, and his mouth opens to make a sarcastic comment. "We are adults."

"Kids at heart, though."

He rests his hand over his heart as I roll my eyes again and smile.

"Let's just start working and then order food before I get hangry."

Tobias grins and then rubs his chin, a slow smile creeping onto his lips.

"I better order the pizza now. You aren't going to enjoy working with me tonight."

"Why not?" I ask.

"Because." He reaches for the back of his neck. "I think I forgot how to write."

"You didn't forget how to write." I sit beside him.

"Are you sure? Because I haven't finished a book in two years. Two years, Nat. What does that say about me?"

"Really bad writer's block?" I ask with a shrug. "Have you talked to the guys about it yet?"

He shakes his head.

"I've started to a couple of times but never go through with it."

"Why?"

He runs a hand through his plush hair. "Their lives are all … flourishing. I don't want to bring them down."

"You need to tell them," I say softly.

Tobias confessed to me about eight months ago that he was having a tough time writing. I wish I had the solution for him.

Holding it in, though, is not a good idea.

"I will."

"Soon." I let my voice grow stern as I stare him down. "They might not have the answers, but they will understand and find a way to help. They're your best friends, Tobias. Tell them."

"I have only one best friend," he says, pointing his pen at me. "And she knows about it."

"You know what I mean."

He sighs, sliding his computer in front of him and opening it.

I snap it closed.

"Okay, wait, let's think. What happened two years ago? What were you writing, and what were you doing in life? Let's find the moment that started this … problem."

His lips twist as he thinks. "I don't know. I was working on that small-town billionaire's series, and the final book had just been released, and I was just living life."

"Come on. Think harder. Be more specific. It can't be that difficult. Two years ago, I was selling my house and moving in with Griffin, Nora and I were rebranding the company, and you were on a book tour that fall. Maybe something happened during that trip."

I wait for him to come up with something, but he just

stares at me. His eyes narrow briefly before he looks away to open his computer again.

"You've really been living with Griffin for two years?"

I nod. "Yes, and now we're getting married. It's a normal line of events."

"Yeah." He rubs his chin again. "It's still just crazy to me."

"You know what's crazy to me?" I say quickly. "That you and Griffin aren't friends yet."

"We have nothing in common."

"Um, hello?" I point to myself. "You have me."

"That's where it ends."

I sigh. After four years, I would have assumed that my best friend and boyfriend, now fiancé, would have become friends, but no. Griffin is stuck on Tobias secretly being in love with me, and, well, I've told him about it enough times, and I'm sure that's why he has a tarnished image of Griffin.

I unzip my laptop bag and pull out my MacBook, ready to get to work. It's probably best we change the subject anyway. If they were going to make it happen, one of them would have by now, right?

I log into our company dashboard and have just pulled up Tobias's account when he knocks on the table beside my keyboard.

"Hey." He smiles when I look up.

"Hi."

"If you want me to be his friend, I'll put in more effort."

"You will?" I ask and beam a smile. "Really?"

He nods. "If that will make you happy. I should have done this a long time ago."

"Oh, it will. I can't imagine going through the rest of my life with my bestie and fiancé, not friends."

"Well, rest assured, if I can help it, that is the case no more."

"Thank you."

I wish I could say that Griffin is just as eager to make me happy when it comes to Tobias, but I get it. For years, people have assumed there is more between us. Our relationship is one-of-a-kind. It's hard to explain, but at the end of the day, Tobias and I are just friends, and we will always be there for each other.

"Speaking of Griffin," I start, using this as my segue. I clear my throat. "Can you come with me this weekend to Lovers Lodge?"

"For what?"

"To view the rooms for the ceremony and reception."

"Don't you need your fiancé for that?"

I nod once. "He'll be there. He gets back tonight but then leaves Sunday for work again."

"He knows your engagement party is next weekend, right?"

"He will be back by then, too."

"Does it bother you that he travels this much for work?"

"You're trying to change the topic, but I won't let you. Please come with us."

He huffs out a laugh. "Why do you need me to come with you and Griffin? Won't that be—oh shit, Nat, really? Is his sister going?"

I look everywhere but at him.

"Nat. Answer me."

"His mom couldn't make it, so his sister is going, and yes, I need you there to help distract her."

He leans back, crossing his arms. "Look me in the eye when you ask me."

I cringe.

In addition to Griffin's sister being a tad crazy, she's also Tobias's biggest fan ever. Like an ultimate fan. Like one book shy of building a shrine to him in her bedroom kind of fan. Anytime she's around him, she melts and loses her mind. I need this weekend to be Griffin's and my choices, not his mother's, which is precisely the voice his sister will give if it's them against me. Hence Tobias. Still, even I feel bad for him when she's around, so I know this is a big ask.

I slowly look up and bite my lip.

His arms are crossed, and he's shaking his head.

"Please. It's one day. I'll even read another of your books if that makes you say yes."

He laughs. "Wow. You're desperate."

I press my hands together.

"You're my favorite romance writer."

He tosses a paper clip in my face.

"Says the woman who's read only one of my books."

I cringe. But it's true.

Technically, it was half a book, but I can spare him the details.

After his first book came out, Nora read it first. I'll never forget her words: *Don't read this book unless you want more than a friendship with Tobias.* I'll also never forget that I didn't listen. Sure, I waited until he had three or four books released, but she was right. I started a book, and when the sex started—holy moly, dirty talk—I saw only him. He doesn't know that small fact, though. He never will.

I still read romance, just not his.

Now that I'm getting married, though, I should give them another chance.

Heck, he writes such incredibly sexy books that maybe I'd learn something new for the bedroom.

"It was my favorite romance ever," I add to hopefully seal the deal.

"Oh god, here she goes. Let's hear it."

"Hear what? Me begging?"

He nods once. "Yes, I want to hear you beg, Natalie."

His deep voice makes me pause.

I look at him.

He looks at me.

"So, you'll come?" I ask.

"Yep."

"Perfect! I'll pick you up on Saturday at about nine."

"Sounds good. These next two days will be torture waiting for this magical moment."

"Stop." I laugh at his sarcasm.

Okay, one problem solved for me, and now it's his turn.

"Before we discuss my job, let's discuss yours. Tell me about the book you're currently writing."

"Okay, let me just … done. Pizza is ordered."

"Smart." I cross my legs in the chair and rest my chin in my hands. "I'm ready."

"Okay, well, it's a fake marriage slash enemies-to-lovers story."

"Tell me more. That's a hit right now. You should see my Kindle. Everyone loves them, and—right, right, we're talking about your books. Now, keep going. I need to know what happens to this fake couple."

"Well, her ex shows up to get married at the place where she works."

"And so, naturally, her enemy is also there, and he pretends to be in love with her so that her ex knows she's not still pining for him?"

That laugh I love so much fills the room.

"You got it."

"So, what's the problem?"

"I don't know. No chemistry between the characters, I guess."

"You guess? Is there banter, hand brushes, does he touch her lower back, does he—"

"It's all there," he cuts me off. "I think I need to change something with the whole process, but I don't know what."

"Hmm."

I hate that I don't have a solution for him.

"It still blows my mind that you can write all these love stories, and yet you've never decided to settle down," I say instead of making up some crap advice to cheer him up. He'd hate that.

He shrugs and then asks, "Have you been talking to Grandma Betty?"

I shake my head. "No, but Betty is a smart woman. Did you know she just joined Snapchat? Last night, she snapped me a picture of you sitting in a muddy puddle in nothing but your diaper."

"Jesus. I should never have introduced you two."

"Mud looks good on you."

"Everything looks good on me."

I fake a gag, and then we get to work on his social media platform scheduling.

Tobias is a fantastic romance writer. I could tell him this over and over until his ears bleed from listening to me, but I also know him well enough to know that wherever is going on with him, he needs to come to terms with how to solve it on his own.

About twelve posts and one pizza down later, I grab the pint of chocolate chip cookie dough from his freezer and sit on the edge of the table. My gaze drifts to the small stack of nonfiction books he keeps around to enhance his writing craft. The one with two names on it sparks an idea.

"Hey, what if the change you need is to co-write a book?"

He pauses, his gaze snagging on my bare legs for a split moment.

"Co-write a book. With whom?"

"Me," I say. "I told you I wanted to write a book the day I met you. I would be such a fun writing partner. I have no expectations of this business, so no pressure, you know."

"No."

I tap his thigh with my foot.

"Come on, it could be fun. Plus, that would mean you're stuck with me forever. Even after I'm married."

He stands to grab the other pint of ice cream, watching me closely.

"Is that something you're worried about? That I'll disappear once you're married?"

I shake my head instead of answering right away.

I didn't think it was, but the words fell from my lips so easily that maybe it is.

"No, of course not. I just ... you said you wanted to do

something different, and I'd love to write a book. It was just an idea."

"I'll think about it."

"Really?"

"Yeah."

I smile and sit back down, but something feels off.

Tobias walks behind me to get to his seat but stops, wraps an arm around me to hug me from behind, and kisses the top of my head.

When he joins me at the table again, I sneak a glance his way. Once upon a time, he always went with his gut. He made choices right and left without thinking about them. Now, he doesn't know what direction to go with anything in his writing life.

I've always known how to help him, but today I don't.

Maybe I'm not afraid to lose him after I get married. Perhaps I'm worried that I already am.

CHAPTER THREE
TOBIAS

I've always had trouble sleeping, even as a kid. I was never the type to sleep for long periods of time. I'd fall asleep late and wake up early. I can get five hours of sleep in a night and feel like I slept ten or more. My energy has never lacked, and I don't spend my days drinking coffee to keep the momentum up.

I'm sure most of that is thanks to my grandmother, or Grandma Betty as I call her. I'm not saying there's something wrong with kids these days, but the older generations know what hard work looks like and what not giving up means.

I love that I was raised that way. I owe a lot of my success to it.

It's probably why I've been up the last two hours hitting my daily word count and then deleting it, approving next month's copy Nat and I created a couple of nights ago for my social media, and reviewing the six new possible real estate options Simon sent me for our next location—all before seven in the morning.

None of these locations are bad per se, but the two that are within walking distance from other venues or restaurants pull my attention more. People are prone to pick a place to work based on convenience, and if they have to drive even five miles out of town, despite the size of that space being amazing, it's a drawback. This brings me down to my top two picks.

TOBIAS

I like the Hillsheer Avenue one that splits up the room. We could put meeting tables and chairs on one side. Consider adding an additional rent cost to book it.

SIMON

I haven't had coffee yet, but I like the one with the apartment over it.

TOBIAS

Are you thinking of renting it out?

SIMON

It's an option. Or a place for us to crash when we're there.

TOBIAS

Which would be rare. We could renovate it and make it a private space.

SIMON

Do we want that added expense?

I rub my chin. It would make sense for me to call him, but he has a point, and it's still early. I click on the property he likes and look at the pictures again. It's a beautiful apartment—red brick in all the right spots and very industrial-looking. Honestly, it's just my style if I were to have a downtown property. It would probably be easy to rent out once we didn't need it. Who could say no to potential passive income?

I'm about to text Simon back when my phone rings, and Grandma Betty's face appears on the screen. I showed her FaceTime once the day before I started college, and she's never called me the original way since.

I press the green button, and before I have a chance to get the first word off my lips, she beats me to it.

"Where is your shirt?" she asks.

Even though it's clear that she can see me, I can see only her feet as she walks through her house.

"Grandma, you have to switch the camera around so I can see your face."

"I'm still in my pajamas."

"So?"

"So, that's about the same thing as looking at you right now. Now, I know you're probably wearing shorts, but dear, it could appear as if I were talking to my grandson naked."

I roll my eyes, heading for my room to grab a shirt. "I'm not naked, Grandma."

Even in my thirties, I feel like I'm in trouble and need to explain myself.

"Good. You might live alone, but there is no need for that. Please wear some underwear at the very least."

I chuckle and then set the phone down to pull on a navy blue shirt with my latest series logo.

"Better?" I ask as I make my way back to the kitchen.

"Much. Thank you. You've always been a good listener."

I shake my head. She's not wrong. I've always respected my grandparents and parents. Even when I was a young kid, my parents would comment on how lucky they were. My well-behaved manner is probably why, when my parents decided to move to North Carolina the summer before my senior year of high school, my grandma didn't even hesitate to let me move in with her so I could graduate with my friends and start college here in Wind Valley, hence why she's a big part of why I act the way I do.

We've always had a good relationship, but that year, as silly as it might sound, Grandma Betty became more than my grandma—she became the most important person in my life.

"Well, you taught me well," I say, grabbing an overnight oats meal I prepared last night and sitting at the table.

"Is that so? Then why is Natalie's engagement party next weekend with another man?"

I blow a raspberry and prop my phone up. Grandma finally flips the phone around and does the same as she eats her breakfast. A small yogurt is all she picked for today.

"Grandma, we've been over this."

"I know. For *years*. Now, I'm not a fan of homewreckers, Tobias Sebastian Banks, but we both know you and Natalie belong together."

"We don't know that. She's happy. And we're just friends, Grandma."

Typically, our conversations are about my books and her newest sewing adventure, but ever since Natalie got engaged, she has brought her up in every conversation we have.

Even before I answer her calls, I know that's the topic, but this is Grandma Betty. I'd never ignore her.

"Mm, maybe so, but she'd be happier with you."

"We're *just friends*," I repeat.

"It makes me sad when you lie."

"I'm not lying," I say through another laugh. "How's Mr. Tinder from next door?"

Her spoon drops into her yogurt cup.

"Stop calling him that."

"Well, coming to your house to ask you if he set up his dating profile right, then showing you all of it is a major pickup move if I ever saw one."

"It wasn't even Tinder."

I chuckle as her cheeks turn a rosy color.

"Wait, do you like him?"

"No."

"Grandma! You have a crush."

"This phone call isn't about me."

"It is now."

She shakes her head.

"I'll be in Lovers this weekend. Nat and I will be at the lodge looking at the spaces for the wedding."

Grandma perks up in her chair.

"Just the two of you?"

"No, her fiancé is coming too. And his sister."

She huffs. "I'll stop by."

"Be nice, Grandma."

"I'm always nice."

My grin is my only reply.

"I'll see you later, dear. I love you."

"I love you too."

Silence fills my kitchen as soon as she hangs up.

Even my grandmother has a busier dating life than me.

I sit back, take a bite, and then look at my laptop.

Shit, is this a sign that dating again is the direction I need to go?

I mean, I date, but no one has ever sparked anything inside me to ask for a second date. I don't see the point if I don't see it going anywhere.

Why chance hurting someone when I know after one day?

I push the thought of dating from my mind and head for the shower.

Dating is out of the question until I figure out my career.

How do I fix it?

I have no idea.

* * *

"I knew I'd find you here," Simon says, walking into The Space. "Out of all of us, you have a house to yourself, and yet you're still here the most."

I lean back and gesture to the expansive open room. "I think the fact that other people are here getting shit done motivates me."

"That makes sense." He sets his stuff down and joins me. "Did you get past that scene you were struggling with the other day?"

"Ah, that would be no. I moved on to another book."

"Again? What the hell, Tobias? What's going on with you? Are you about to pull some big reveal of releasing a book a month for a year or what?"

I could see how he'd think that since I've held back the truth.

"I know it. You're like six books ahead of me now. Shit," I

say the words in a joking tone to pull the attention off me. It works.

He chuckles. "It's not a competition."

"No, but it's like the longer I go between releases, the more I feel out of sync with the industry. So much is changing, and I'm stuck here." I gesture to my computer with my hands. "I don't even know where here is."

Well, shit. That's the most I've divulged to someone who isn't Natalie.

Simon studies me briefly before asking, "Do you not enjoy it anymore?"

"I do. I love writing. I still write every day, but I think I get bored."

"Did you talk to Natalie about it? She's always been a good source for you. You two are more in sync than anyone I know. She could basically write a book about you at this point."

I eye him carefully.

"Did she say something to you?"

"About what?"

"Writing a book."

He shakes his head.

"Oh, well, she suggested we write one together to help me get out of my funk."

His left brow peaks. "Really? What did you say?"

"That I would think about it."

"What's holding you back?"

"I write smut. Can you imagine Nat and I writing that together? Yeah, we've talked about sex before, but writing it out explicitly would be different."

"You're both professionals. I'm sure you can get past it."

I roll my eyes and shake my head.

"I just can't do it."

"Because you think of her as more than a friend?"

"No," I snap.

"Sorry!" He holds his hands up. "I know she's a touchy subject."

"I just wish you guys would accept that we're only friends. Hell, she and *Griffin* are getting married in a matter of months."

"Why did you say his name like that?"

"Like what?"

"*Griffin*," he says with a shake of his shoulders.

"I didn't say it like that."

"You did."

I sigh. "I don't know. Do you like him?"

Simon smirks. "I don't think that matters. It matters if Natalie likes him."

"He's gone a lot."

"Okay."

"Like *a lot*." I close my computer. "And he wanted to get married fast."

"Okay. Nothing wrong with being so in love that you want to seal the deal quickly."

I glare at him.

"He's a nice guy, Tobias. What's going on in your head?"

"He's too nice, though, right? Always saying the right thing and magically has something in common with all of you."

"He's social. It's not a crime."

"He's too perfect. There has to be something wrong with him."

Simon sighs, now closing his computer, too. "Maybe you just don't like him because Natalie spends more time with him than you these days."

Ouch. He's not wrong.

Is that it?

I blow out a breath. "She asked me to try being his friend."

"Makes sense."

"I said I would, but I don't know if I can."

Simon doesn't say anything more. He just watches me.

"I'm going to try."

"Are you?"

"Yes, Natalie wants me to."

"Okay, so what's the problem?" he asks with a slight chuckle. "I don't mean to be a dick, but he seems like a nice guy and Natalie is happy. What more are you looking for?"

I twist my mouth and think about my answer.

"I don't know," I say and lean back.

And I'm so sick and tired of not knowing anything these days.

* * *

"Heyyyyyy, Tobias!"

"What the fuck, Natalie?" I glare as she holds my front door open for me the following day. "Are you serious right now?"

Griffin is parked on the side of the street, and his sister is leaning out the window behind him, waving at me like I can't see her. Both her arms are flailing about as if she were on a deserted island and trying to flag down a plane flying over.

"We get to ride together," she shouts.

"Did I forget to mention that we're all riding together?" Natalie asks.

We start down the sidewalk together, and under my breath, I say, "I can't believe you're trapping me in a car with her."

"It's going to be fine."

I glare at my so-called best friend before she climbs into the passenger seat. I get into the back.

"Hi," Griffin's sister, Cassie, beams a smile at me.

A stack of special edition copies of my books sits on her lap.

"I have something for you to do to kill time on our road trip," she says.

Natalie peeks around her seat, failing to hide her smile.

"This is great, Cassie. Thank you," I say and grab the first book she hands me. "I don't have a pen, though."

She holds up a bag that has maybe ten inside of it.

"I've got you covered."

"Perfect."

I look up at Griffin to say hello to him, but he's holding his phone to his ear.

Has he not heard of Bluetooth? I bet his car has it.

The conversation must be private. But come on, Nat's in the car. He needs to be focused when he drives. Especially for a couple of hours.

"Can you make them all out to Cassie with a private note?"

Oh, and his sister is here too.

We fall into a rhythm of me signing books and her cooing over my notes for the next half hour. When her phone rings, I take this opportunity to text Natalie. I might be going through a stage of life when I question everything, but there is one thing I know for sure.

TOBIAS

After this road trip, this friendship is over.

NATALIE

You're so sweet to her. #friendsforever

TOBIAS

She's a grown woman, Natalie.

NATALIE

Ask her out.

"For fuck's sake," I say out loud, and Natalie snorts from the front seat.

"Are you okay?" Griffin asks. He got off the phone about five minutes ago and gave me a measly *hello, Tobias.* That was it. Like I said, he's not a fan of mine.

But that's okay. He can be a dick to me. As long as Natalie is happy, I truly don't care.

"Can you draw a heart in this one?" Cassie asks quickly to rein me back to her presence.

That's how the car ride goes until we reach Lovers Lodge.

I can't get out of the car fast enough, and it seems neither can Griffin. He's locking the vehicle and walking briskly toward the main entrance. His sister is hot on his heels, leaving Natalie and me trailing behind.

He should be walking next to his fiancée. Or holding her hand, and they should be gushing over their wedding venue.

But no, he disappears inside.

Making friends with someone like that is definitely at the top of my to-do list. *Not.*

I glance at Natalie, who is looking at me with a smile.

"Thank you for coming with me," she says, and her smile widens.

"Anytime." I swing my arm over her shoulders, leading her inside.

Heck, if Griffin's behavior doesn't bother her and she's still smiling, I won't let it get to me.

Even if I think she deserves better than him.

CHAPTER FOUR

NATALIE

"And this room is where we would host the reception," the Lovers Lodge wedding planner says as we walk into a large room already set up for a wedding this evening. It's clear that the tables, the dance floor, and the stage were made for this room to hold significant events.

"It's great. I love the flow it has moving from the ceremony to the reception. I think the guests are going to love this," Griffin says, really laying his joy on thick.

It's beautiful, by all means, but maybe a little big.

"Do we have enough guests to fill this room?" I ask.

"All our friends could fit at one table," Tobias says behind us, and I laugh at his accuracy.

Griffin glares at us and clears his throat.

Tobias walks off to join Cassie, who is moving the plates around on one of the tables.

"I don't think the guest size matters," Griffin finally adds, smiling at the wedding planner. "This place is beautiful."

"Ooh, we could practice dancing. See if the floor is ready

to go," Cassie cheers from behind us. She reaches for Tobias. He flinches, jerking his hands from her reach, but he doesn't move his feet.

I do feel bad for putting him in this position today, but Cassie has been so distracted by him that it's been me, Griffin, and the wedding planner most of the time we have been here. The only suggestions today, even if they have been opposite of what I'd have liked, have been mine and my fiancé's. Not his mom's or his sister's.

My goal here has been accomplished.

I owe Tobias big.

Like helping him find a solution to his writing problem, big. I wish he'd share more with me, but I think that's a writer thing. They don't always like to share when they feel like they are failing.

Still, Tobias used to share every detail of his life with me.

Shoot, I know everything about him.

Right now, I know he wants to bail—run out of here and happily pay a stranger to drive him back to Wind Valley. He hates situations where he doesn't call the shots or has people obsess over him like he's a prince or something. It's why he stopped doing book signings last year. He's not a fan of attention.

Still, he's doing it for me, and I love him even more for that.

Cassie tries to do some kind of twirl move, resulting in her kneeing Tobias in the groin, and I have to look away. If we make eye contact, he will murder me with his gaze.

"How cool would it be if Tobias and Cassie hit it off?" Griffin leans in to whisper in my ear.

I snort out a laugh, and he glares at me. "Oh, you were serious?"

He nods.

"I don't think Tobias is the commitment type. I've told you this. I wouldn't want him breaking her heart."

It's all true. Mostly. It's true, I've never seen him in a real relationship, but I think it's just because he doesn't want one. The breaking her heart part is extra accurate.

Griffin nods. "Cassie likes just to have fun, too. I think they'd hit it off. She looks like his type."

"His type?"

"Yeah. Look at her."

And I do. I see long blonde hair, a small waist, lean legs, and breasts that are probably four times the size of mine.

Is that his type?

"If you think that's his type, then why do you constantly ask me if he likes me? I look nothing like your sister."

Griffin pauses to stare at me. "That's a Good point. Not to mention, they're both wild and fun. Now that I think of it, you really aren't his type."

"Are you saying I'm not fun?"

"I didn't say that."

"It sounded like it."

Griffin glances between me and Tobias and then turns his focus back to the wedding planner.

"Stop," I say. "I know what you're thinking."

"I'm not thinking that. I'm thinking that maybe I've been too harsh in accusing you two of being more than you are. For that, I am sorry."

"Really?" I press up to my toes to kiss him, but he turns his cheek.

"We're in public, Natalie."

I swallow and nod.

"I know, but it's just us and them." I point to his sister and Tobias.

Of course, Tobias is watching us with a scowl. He's probably ready to get the hell out of here, and after the moment Griffin and I just had, so am I.

"And the wedding planner," Griffin whispers.

Before I can respond, he turns to her and asks, "What options do we have for flowers and dining? We should probably check this all off now so that we can book it before it's too late."

My attention falls back on the dancing duo behind me.

They look like they are having fun.

Fun.

Cassie and Tobias, that's absurd. How could Griffin even think of that?

"Hello, hello!" A familiar voice floats through the room, putting a smile back on my face and pulling me to the entrance like a magnet.

"Grandma Betty!" I pull her into a hug. She squeezes me tight and then looks around the room.

"This place is so beautiful, Natalie."

I hear the hesitation in her voice.

"But …" I encourage her.

"Doesn't it feel a bit big?"

"That's what I said."

"Natalie," Griffin calls. "Hi, Betty."

"Griffin, it's lovely to see you."

"Hi, Grandma," Tobias comes up and hugs her as I drift back to where I'm needed.

"Here is the menu and the flier for the local bakery and flower shop," he says, handing them to me. "I'm going to go look at our options for room blocks."

"Okay," I say to his retreating back. I glance down at the pamphlets; the pictures of the cake alone are making me hungry.

Cassie starts to follow her brother, leaving me, Tobias, and Grandma Betty alone in the room.

"Don't you need to go with them?" Tobias asks.

I glance at the entrance doors.

"Nope. I'm good right here," I say, walking back to chat more with Grandma Betty.

"Are you okay?" Tobias asks softly.

"I'm good."

But really, I'm not so sure I am. I should be running out behind Griffin to pick out all the wedding things, right?

Instead, I'd rather stay right here.

Listening to Grandma Betty scold Tobias for his untucked shirt and listening to him laugh when she teases him.

Will I still get moments like this after I'm married?

* * *

The afternoon in Lovers ran longer than expected, but I think I can speak for most of us in the car and say that the sight of Cassie asleep has been the best part of the day.

"Are you happy with the venue?" Griffin whispers.

I almost laugh—even he doesn't want to wake his sister.

I nod. "Are you sure it's not too big?"

"It's perfect. Plus, we will be so busy enjoying the day

that we won't notice the size of the room. Just the people in it."

"Us." I smile.

"And our families, friends, and colleagues."

Right, the colleagues.

I gaze over my shoulder at Tobias, who is clearly watching me, but he quickly looks away.

"Thank you for coming."

"Of course."

I quickly look between him and Griffin, hoping he will pick up on my hint.

His eye roll says that he does.

"So, Griffin," he starts, sitting forward in the car as far as his seat belt will let him go. "How long are you in town for?"

"I leave tomorrow."

"Oh."

His gaze drifts to me.

I widen my eyes. *Go on.*

"I was thinking we should get a drink sometime and hang out."

I bite my lip, my eyes on Tobias for a moment before I look at Griffin.

He doesn't give anything away with his expression.

"Okay. I'll reach out when I get back."

"Great."

I do a little cheer inside and grab my phone to text Tobias.

NATALIE

Thank you.

TOBIAS

Anything for you.

. . .

And then I let out a breath.

Tobias and Griffin are going to become friends, and all will be right in my world.

I'll still get them both.

For the first time since the night at Tobias's house, where he said he'd try, I feel like I can breathe again.

Lose my best friend because I'm getting married.

Ha.

That will never happen.

CHAPTER FIVE
TOBIAS

Do you know how some people look like animals?

I don't mean it in a cruel way, but more in why do I look at this girl and think I see a bird, or why does that old man make me think of a turtle?

The longer I look at Griffin's picture in the one Natalie posted of her with him outside Lovers Lodge, the more I see a giraffe. A baby giraffe, like he's trying so hard to extend his neck to show how tall he is.

It's that or the fact that somewhere over the last four years, I have grown to dislike the man.

At first, he seemed pretty cool. Nat would laugh a lot around him. She'd come over swooning over him and the fact he sent flowers to her on the first of every month. Or that he surprised her with date nights when she didn't even know he was back in town.

She was happy, and I was happy for her. Then they got serious. Nat and I still hung out a lot, but it was less and less often as time went on.

Perhaps I dislike him for the sole fact that he's taking away the one constant in my life. Between that and this book, life sort of sucks right now.

Still, as every day goes by and it gets closer to their wedding, I find myself finding more and more reasons to dislike him. And it's not because he's stealing Natalie from me.

I know it's not.

Take, for example, tonight. He's going to fly in from California and drive straight to meet me for a beer.

He's not going home to shower or unwind. He didn't suggest another night after he hadn't been traveling. And he sure as hell didn't say another night was better because he wanted to be with Natalie after being away for two days.

What man in love does that? I might not be an expert from experience, but I know plenty of men who are.

I pull up a group text.

Tobias

You're two nights away from your girl, and the only thing you want when you get back is to meet another guy for a beer. Yay or nay?

Surprisingly, they all answer swiftly.

BECK

Is this a real question?

ZANE

Is this where you're stuck in your story?

GRAHAM

I ... what?

HERO

What's happening?

SIMON

Is this about Griffin again?

I glance up at the bar to make sure he isn't here yet. What fun that would be to have him catch me talking shit. He'd love to run back to Nat with that information.

Tobias

Yes, this is about Griffin. He suggested we meet tonight. He's coming to the Black Alcove before he even goes home to see Nat. He's been gone two days.

HERO

Ahh, I see. Okay, nay. One day away from Nora, and I can't take it.

BECK

Same. A couple of hours away from Calla and I'm (Simon, skip ahead so you don't read something dirty about your sister) ready to strip her down and refuse to leave our bed for weeks.

SIMON

insert middle finger emoji

But yeah, okay, I do find this odd. How
does Natalie feel?

TOBIAS

I don't know. That's a weird question to ask
her. She'd probably have a lot of follow-up
questions I don't have answers to.

GRAHAM

Nay for me too.

"Writing a book on your phone?" Griffin's voice pulls me
from the screen. I close the thread quickly and set it face
down.

"Something like that." I smile.

He sighs heavily as if he would rather be anywhere else in
the world. He even stands at the end of the table like he's
going to change his mind. After an awkward minute, he
shrugs off his coat and sits across from me.

"What's up?" he asks.

Shit. I made the effort and set up the time, but did I plan
what we would actually talk about? Nope.

"Same old, same old. How was your flight?"

Yeah, that's a good, safe question.

"Is that really what you want to ask me?"

"Yes?"

His brow peaks.

"Look, I'll be honest. Natalie asked me to make an effort.
You mean a lot to her, and she means a lot to me, so here I
am. Let's give our girl some peace of mind and find a

common ground."

He rubs his chin and leans back. His phone rings, so he takes it out and answers it.

Okay, rude, but we aren't exactly besties.

"Hi … yeah, I made it … good, did you get them? You liked them? Good," he says, and then looks up at me. "I'll call you when I get done here. I don't know. Ten minutes."

Jesus.

He hangs up.

"Natalie?" I ask, for god knows what reason.

His eyes narrow as he takes me in, and he places the phone on the table.

"All right, first, I think you meant to say *my girl*, not *our girl*, and two, I—"

"It's actually second," I interrupt.

"What?"

"Well, you said first and then made a statement, so your follow-up would be second, not two. Unless you said one, she's not my girl" —*excuse me while I mentally punch him*— "and two, then made your—"

"I don't care," he cuts me off.

Noted.

"Are you in love with Natalie or not?" he asks. "If you are, then I suggest you back off and let her be. Do you want to hurt her?"

Well, this was not the conversation I was expecting. Also, who the fuck is this guy? Is this how he presents himself to Natalie?

Not fucking okay. Not one bit.

I fold my arms and lean onto the table in front of me.

"Do *you* want to hurt her?" I ask.

"Can I get you two anything to drink?" our waitress asks.

Griffin smirks at her and winks.

Oh, hell no.

Natalie is not marrying this guy. No fucking way. I'm not letting it happen.

As he's flirting with the waitress, his phone buzzes on the table, and a text drops down.

MY LOVE

Baby, I miss you.

I look at the text, and then I look at him. Is that Natalie?

The waitress leaves, and I lean back.

"Come on, man," Griffin goes on. "Admit defeat. I got the girl, and you didn't."

"First of all, she's not a fucking prize."

If I weren't so pissed, I'd laugh, because nowhere in my life did I think I'd ever use that line outside of romance novels.

"*Second*, I'm her best friend. Nothing will change that, so like I said, she wants us to be friends. I'm here to make that happen."

"It won't happen."

He gets up just as the waitress returns with two beers.

"You can get this, right?" Griffin looks at me, and I swear to god, I want to punch this jack-off in the face.

Of course, for Nat, I keep my ass in my chair.

Here I thought I was coming for a "let's be friends" beer.

Well, the joke's on me. This guy shows up thinking he can scare me away from the most important person in my life.

News flash, Griffin. That won't happen.

Natalie Miller deserves better than you, and I'm about to tell her.

CHAPTER SIX
NATALIE

Nora hands me a glass of wine as soon as I've set up my things in her home office. Hero is out of town for the night at a signing a few hours away, so in order for her to avoid a babysitter, I agreed to work at her place tonight.

Nora Quinn and I run a marketing company for authors. We work closely with both publishing houses and independent authors. Nora started this business right out of college, and since I was still a bit undecided on what I wanted to do with my degree in marketing, she took me on as an assistant until I could figure it out. I originally thought it would be easier to be hired by a big company that guarantees a salary than to create my own business and venture into the unknown. Turns out, the unknown kicks ass when it involves something you love.

Plus, a part of me thought I'd have joined the author side of this world by this point.

Tonight is just a meeting, no actual client work, so we'll drink wine. Or rather, I'll drink wine while Nora chugs water.

We try to get together at least once a week to plan and

keep our schedules lined up. Tonight is that night. Griffin is coming in on a late flight, so it made sense to work.

I glance into my cup and realize it's almost full. Is this on purpose, or was she distracted?

"Did you get any sleep last night?" I ask, taking a sip as she sits down with a big sigh. I don't really care about how much is in here—I'm drinking it just the way she gave it to me.

"Yes, but I still can't seem to get adjusted to waking up all through the night. It's almost as if the moment she sets a new sleep schedule and I get used to it, she sets a new one and the process repeats over and over and over. I'll get it figured out, though. No need to worry."

"I can stay longer tonight to babysit if you want a nap," I offer and then open my computer.

She's quiet, so I turn to see what she's doing. She's staring blankly at the wall behind me.

"Nora." I wave a hand in front of her.

She blinks and then laughs.

"Thank you, but I'm okay today. Another day though, I might take you up on that."

"Well, I'll be here for a couple of hours. Plenty of time for you to change your mind."

She grabs one of the cookies I brought.

"This is reward enough. Did you see the new copy Tobias sent over yesterday morning at like six in the morning? Does he even sleep?"

Less now that it seems he can't figure out his writing career. I want to bring up the co-writing thing again, but I don't want to stress him out. It just seems like a good way for him to get out of his box.

Plus, I just keep thinking about how writing was always something I wanted to try. Initially, I thought I'd do it alone, but the more I think about it, the more I want to do it with Tobias.

"Barely," I answer Nora's question. "But yeah, I was up, too, and already scheduled them. Well, as far out as I could. We did a bunch the other night."

"Damn. Am I slacking too much? Do you feel like you have to do both of our jobs and still make time to check out venues?"

"Not at all." I shake my head. "Besides managing schedules for our employees, we have maybe ten clients between the two of us. It's nothing."

The day Nora and I decided to hire more employees, we both agreed on the clients we would keep, and Tobias was at the top of my list.

"You'd tell me, though, right? If you felt like I wasn't holding up."

"Yes, I would."

"Swear it."

"Yes, I swear," I say with a laugh.

"Okay, because I feel like I should be taking on more so you can plan your wedding. How did the venue visit go?"

"Good. We booked it for this winter."

She grins and then grabs a box next to her, handing it to me.

"What is this?"

"Nothing really, just an idea for your bachelorette party."

I grin and take the box. I completely forgot about the bachelorette party. I wonder if Griffin is having a bachelor party. He's shown me the plans for everything, and those parties weren't listed. Maybe because they're a given?

I pull the white bow off and untie the ribbon.

Inside sits a postcard with a picture of the Maldives on it. I pick it up and flip it over.

Pick a date and we are going! Love, Nora, Willa, Calla, Paige, and Greer!

"What is this?"

"It's where we should go for your party. Although, at this point, it'll just be a small group including your sister, and there won't be too much partying. Just lots of cocktails in the sun and relaxation. Isn't this where you've always wanted to go?"

"Yes," I blurt out. "It's been a dream for so long to go there, but that's a lot for a party for me or whatever we want to call it. I can't let anyone pay for this."

"Actually, that's just our excuse. The girls and I decided we needed a reason for a girl's trip there."

I raise my hand. "I'll gladly be the reason. Wow. How did you even know about this?"

Nora and I share a lot, but I don't think we have ever talked about this.

"Look." I point to a small building in the picture. "I think this is even the resort I picked years ago."

"I know."

"How?" I asked again and hug her.

She clears her throat.

"Tobias told me. I asked him what he thought you might like, since I'm a horrible friend who has been so busy lately, and he said he had a postcard. I know it's lame that I didn't even think of it, but he wasn't wrong."

The smile on my face grows. Why did he have a postcard?

Not that I'm complaining, but wow.

I hug her once more.

"You're not a bad friend. Never ever. The best of friends are those who can live their busy lives and still love each other as if nothing has changed."

She tears up and then fans her face, and I stick my bottom lip out. "We will circle back to this, but do you want to change the subject?"

"Yes." She swipes the tears away. "Tell me about wedding planning."

"I was thinking more about work."

She waves her hand around. "We have plenty of time for that. What's it like having Griffin plan most of everything?"

I'm not saying guys aren't into wedding planning, but the way Griffin took the planning by the horns—well, I feel like I should be more upset he's doing more than me, but I'm not. Like I said, maybe I'm not a big wedding type of girl.

"It's good. He's got his checklist, and he's happy as a clam."

She studies me a moment and then crosses her arms.

"What's going on?" she asks.

"Nothing. What do you mean?"

"Are you not excited about getting married?"

"Oh, of course I am. I just ... he's so happy planning it all that I don't mind."

She nods slowly.

"Do you think it's weird?"

"Him planning our wedding?" I ask for more clarity.

"That you're fine not having control."

I shake my head slowly. "I'm okay with it."

She keeps her eyes on me but doesn't say anything else.

My phone chirps, and I glance at the clock. It's six, and that means Griffin is probably about to board his flight and is texting me to check in. It's like clockwork. He's so predictable, I never have to worry. He's probably going to ask me about work.

GRIFF

How's it going at work?

I stare at his text. I've never had a problem with his texts until right now. Even so, I don't have a *problem* problem. He's just asking about my day, but it would be cute if he used a nickname for me or used an emoji. Wait … does he even have a nickname for me?

NATALIE

Good. Do you have a nickname for me?

GRIFF

A nickname? Why would I need one? Your name is beautiful just the way it is, Natalie.

I purse my lips and tilt my head. It's not a bad answer; it's just not what I was looking for.

NATALIE

I have you on my phone as Griff.

GRIFF

Okay. Love you. See you when I land.

I huff and put my phone down.

"Is everything okay?" Nora asks.

"Yes. I just … did you get weird about things and over-think everything before you and Hero got married?"

"Like cold feet?"

Oh, wow. Maybe that's what's wrong with me. Cold feet. Duh.

"Yeah, like cold feet."

She thinks for a moment and then shakes her head. "Nope. I knew he was it for me. Why? Are you getting second thoughts?"

She twists in her seat, giving me her full attention.

"No," I answer. It feels wrong to even think I could give her a different answer. "I think I just miss Griffin is all. He's been traveling a lot. His current flight lands back here late tonight, and then he has one more trip that's basically a fly there, have a meeting, and fly back. He'll get home two hours before the party this weekend."

"That's cutting it close."

"Yeah."

"A little risky for Griffin if you ask me."

I laugh. Her remark is more accurate than she knows.

But then it hits me.

If that's Griffin and he's the one I'm going to marry, that's going to be me too.

No surprises.

No risks.

No *fun*.

Just boring plans and schedules forever.

Have I become boring?

"I'm not saying this is you, but if you are having cold feet, it's normal. Don't stress it, okay? If you love him and he loves you, no matter what, you're going to be happy."

I swallow back any possible tears.

Cold feet.

That's all this is.

It makes the most sense.

* * *

Griffin's truck is in the driveway when I get home. I wasn't expecting him for a couple of more hours, so I hurry inside.

As soon as I step through the doorway, I freeze and suck in a breath.

Flowers line the living room, and Griffin is waiting on the couch.

"What is this?" I ask.

"Oh, I just wanted to surprise you. I hate that I've been gone so much lately."

I rush to him and pull him in for a hug.

"This is amazing."

"It's also my apology."

"For what?"

"My flight got rescheduled to first thing in the morning."

"Oh."

"Yeah, I'm sorry. I just wanted to come home and have one night with you. I'm so ready to crash. Should we get—"

He's cut off by my cell phone. I pull it out of my purse to see Tobias calling.

"Before you answer that, I have to tell you something."

The concern in his tone makes me pause.

"What?"

"I met with Tobias tonight. You know, that beer he asked me to get."

"How did it go?"

He grabs my hand and sits on the couch, pulling me with him.

"Look, Natalie, I know he's your friend, but he went into our meetup with an agenda."

"I know." I sigh. "I asked him to make more of an effort to be your friend. Is that weird?"

He shakes his head. "What's weird is, he did the total opposite."

"The opposite?"

"Yeah, he came at me, telling me I wasn't good enough for you and that I needed to end this. He doesn't like me, Natalie. I tried. I swear I tried. I told him that we needed to try for you, but he wanted none of it. He just told me to get bent."

"What? That doesn't sound like Tobias."

"Trust me, I was shocked too. Maybe he's going through something, and he wanted to take it out on me." He sighs. "You care for him, so I'll give him another chance. I just hope whatever he's going through, he doesn't start to take it out on you."

My phone rings again.

"I love you," he says and kisses my forehead. "I'm headed to bed to give you two some privacy to talk."

He heads down the hall, closing our bedroom door when he gets there.

My phone keeps vibrating, so I glance down at the screen and stare at Tobias's face.

My mind is blown right now. I know Tobias hasn't always cared for Griffin, but to just attack him like that … I can't understand it.

"Hello," I say softly.

"Natalie, are you at your house?"

"Yes."

"I'm coming over. We need to talk."

"Now isn't a good time."

"It really can't wait."

"Is this about the drinks you had with Griffin?"

He huffs into the phone.

"Yes."

"He already told me."

"Shit. He did? Are you okay? Wait, what did he say?"

"Does it matter?"

"Yes. It matters. I want to know that he told you the truth."

"And what's the truth?" I ask. It only makes sense that I hear them both out.

"Is he there now?" Tobias asks.

"Yes."

"Fuck. Okay. I didn't want to say this to you over the phone, but I think he's cheating on you."

"What?"

"Yeah, I can't prove it, but I get this feeling that he's doing something shitty, and you deserve better than him."

Oh god. Griffin was right.

"I asked you to make friends with him, Tobias, not fight with him."

"It was hard to—can I just come over? I hate having this conversation over the phone."

I take a breath to hold back the threatening tears.

"Why would you …" I can barely get the words out. "Is this because of the writing thing?"

"What? What are you talking about?"

"Are you acting like this because you're confused and want to vent your frustration on someone else, so you picked Griffin?"

"What? No."

"Because that's a shitty thing to do. He's not cheating on me, Tobias, and it's even shittier of you to make that accusation when, as you said, you don't even have proof."

"Nat, just let me come over so we can talk."

"No. I don't want to be the next person on your list. Just because your life isn't going how you wanted it to doesn't mean you need to bring me down with you."

I place my hand over my heart.

Why would he say something like that to me? Why would he want to hurt me?

"All right, look. I'm not sure what he said to you, but let's talk about it, okay? Maybe you can take the night to cool off and we can talk tomorrow."

"Sure, fine."

"Nat, come on. Talk to me."

"I have to go," I say, hanging up the phone.

My heart is still racing with adrenaline a minute after the call end.

Did he really just say those awful things to Griffin? It's not like him. And then to accuse him of cheating!

I can't …

Then again, it's not like me to say the hurtful things I just said either.

This time, the tears can't be stopped. If I was worried about losing my best friend after I got married, I guess I can stop now.

I'm pretty sure it just happened.

CHAPTER SEVEN
TOBIAS

What's the point of an engagement party?

I stare at the suit I had dry-cleaned earlier this week and run a hand through my hair.

They posted a picture of the ring online to make the announcement and sent out save-the-date cards. People already know it's happening. Not to mention, my group of friends held a little surprise party for Nat the weekend after it happened. It doesn't matter that Griffin was out of town and wasn't there to celebrate—we already did this.

I just don't get it.

Maybe the invitation said more, but I still haven't opened it.

Natalie gave me all the details in person. Reading them seemed pointless. Hello, it's not like I'd forget. I remember everything that woman has ever said to me. Her likes, her dislikes, her dreams and goals, how she broke her leg in fifth grade and pretended she was still healing to get out of track even after her cast was off and she felt great. I couldn't forget anything about her even if I tried.

I blow out a breath.

Which is exactly why her words from the last time we talked, two nights ago, keep playing in my mind.

Just because your life isn't going the way you wanted doesn't mean you need to bring me down with you.

Is that what I've been doing?

Is this why I've been looking for a reason to make Griffin the villain?

I saw the way he looked at that waitress, and my gut still says that "my love" text wasn't from Natalie, but I have no proof.

Just a gut feeling Natalie might have just summed up in one statement. Maybe I am miserable, and I'm looking to put everyone on my level.

Shit, does she even still want me there tonight?

I can't imagine not being there for her.

I guess I'll know my answer when they kick me out or not. Knowing Griffin, he probably will.

I stand, ready to get dressed and put on my best smile for the rest of the night. I've barely removed the coat off the hanger when my phone rings.

It's not a number I recognize. Probably spam, but this sinking feeling in my gut tells me I should answer it.

Or maybe I'll just do anything right now to avoid getting ready for the night.

"Hello?"

"Is this Tobias Banks?" a voice rushes out.

"Yes."

"This is Mike Timmons. I live next door to your grandmother."

My heart rate instantly spikes, and I toss the hanger and coat onto my bed.

"Yeah, okay. Is there a reason you're calling me?"

"She gave me your number in case of emergencies and—"

"Where is she? What happened? Put her on the phone."

"She's fine, she's fine, but she's on her way to Lovers's hospital."

I'm already down my stairs and grabbing my keys before he can say more.

"Why?" I snap into the phone, repeating myself. "What happened?"

"She fell down her stairs, and she's pretty banged up, but because of her age, they took her to monitor her."

"I'm a little over two hours away. Does she have her phone?"

"No, I'm following the ambulance, and I have it with me."

A fucking ambulance for falling? How bad was it?

I don't know this guy, but I sure as hell can guarantee he isn't going to tell me all the details. He'll sugarcoat it. People always do because they don't want anyone to panic.

"If you see her before I get there, tell her I'm on my way."

"I will. See you soon."

My tires peel out of the driveway as I head for the highway between Wind Valley and Lovers.

I press the green phone button on my steering wheel. "Call Hero Quinn."

My car repeats his name back to me and then it rings.

"Hey, man, are you already there?"

"No. I'm … I'm not going to make it." My heart aches.

"Are you kidding me? What's going on?"

"Grandma Betty fell, and she's in an ambulance on her way to the hospital in Lovers."

"Fuck. Okay. Is she all right?"

"Her neighbor said she's fine, but I need to—"

"I'll explain everything to Natalie. She'll understand."

"Actually, don't tell her."

I tap my thumbs on the steering wheel. No one in our group is a big fan of lying, but this is a special case. Or so I tell myself.

"What?"

"I don't want to ruin the party with her worrying about Grandma Betty. We both know she will. She'll probably sit at a table by herself holding her phone and crying or something. This is a big night; I don't want to steal it from her."

"She's going to ask."

The guys don't know about the fight we had, and it's probably best not to share it right now.

"I know. I'm not asking you to lie, but please do your best to not tell her everything."

"Tobias, this … she's going to be mad at you."

I nod even though he can't see me. She will. I know. But our relationship is changing anyway. Maybe it'll be easier for us to back away from each other if she's upset with me.

"I'll explain to her later."

"Are you sure this is what you want to do? She's your best friend."

She is. She always will be, even if she doesn't want to be mine anymore.

"I'm sure."

CHAPTER EIGHT
NATALIE

I should dress up more often.

I smooth my hand over the white strapless dress that's form-fitted to my body and do a spin in the mirror. I had my makeup done for tonight. Well, the professional I hired pretty much used it as a trial for the wedding day, and my hair is down in waves, giving it a whole twenties maybe thirties vibe.

I feel beautiful, and I love it.

"Natalie, are you ready?" Griffin asks, stepping into our room. He smiles from ear to ear. "You look great," he says and kisses my cheek.

"Thank you. Your suit is very sharp."

He stands next to me in the mirror and kisses the top of my head.

"We should go."

He moves quickly, but I stand still. He complimented me, but I don't know. I thought maybe he'd have more of a reaction.

I groan and grab my bag.

I'm totally overthinking everything these days. Is this what getting married is supposed to be like? Questioning every moment, every word, every look from your fiancé?

I totally get why people elope.

The fact that Tobias and I still haven't talked is weighing on me too.

I need to apologize for what I said. I was out of line.

And I need to hear him out.

I meet Griffin at the door, and he follows me out to his car. He opens the door for me, winks at me with another smile, and then walks around to the driver's side.

As soon as we get there, the room is already full of our friends and family. People greet us the minute we walk in. After about twenty minutes, Nora walks by with two champagne glasses, handing them to me and Griffin as he chats with a colleague, his arms around my hips to keep me at his side. I silently thank her and smile at the other guests who wave at me.

"Excuse me," I interrupt my fiancé. "I'm going to go say hello to my family." I hold out my hand to a guy I know he works with, but I cannot remember his name. "It's great to see you again. Thank you for coming."

He gives me a quick hug and a quiet congratulations, and Griffin rubs my back right before I head for my mom, dad, and sister.

"I cannot believe I didn't have a different dress for every event of my wedding," my sister, Lilly, says as wraps her arms around me. "You look smoking hot in this dress. What did Griffin say?"

Not that.

"He likes it too" is how I answer.

"You look lovely, dear," my mother says, and she and my father also hug me.

Maybe this night should be renamed the night of the hugs.

"Have you eaten?" I ask them, noticing their bare table. "It's self-serve appetizers the entire night. Griffin kept it simple so everyone could snack as they like."

"We'll get food soon." My mom smiles at me. "Don't worry about us. I'm sure you have a lot of people to see tonight. I haven't seen Tobias, though. Is he running late?"

"Yeah, I need to talk to him about his next release," Lilly says and fans her face. "Have you read it? Do you know when it is?"

I shake my head. No one knows that we're fighting. Well, at least I haven't told anyone anyway.

"I don't actually. I've been busy."

She grabs my hand to look at my ring again.

"Very."

I scan the room, noticing my friends all gathered at one table, but like my mom said, Tobias isn't there. I look around once more, but there is no sign of him.

A lump forms in my throat. That was our biggest fight to date and the words held weight. I feel sick about it.

"I'm going to see if Nora knows where Tobias is. It's not like him to be late."

"Okay, see you in a bit."

I march straight for the only table of the night who won't demand my attention, my heels clicking on the hard floor announcing a woman on a mission.

"Have you guys seen Tobias?"

Nora looks down. Hero grabs her hand and rubs her back. Slowly, one by one, everyone sitting at the table looks away.

Heat crawls up my spine.

"What? Where is he?"

Simon clears his throat and swirls the bottom of his drink against the table as he looks up. "He's in Lovers."

"Oh. Why is he—Oh god," I gasp. "Is Grandma Betty okay?"

Simon nods.

"All right." I glance at the group again, but still they avoid looking at me. "What's going on?"

This time, it's Zane who clears his throat.

"He …"

"He what, Zane? Spit it out. Someone, anyone, please."

My heart races as I wait for an answer. The way everyone is avoiding me right now, I'm worried something terrible happened to him. Whatever it is, they're afraid to tell me.

"When is he coming back?" I ask when it's clear my last question is going to go unanswered.

Nora shifts out of Hero's embrace to sit next to me. She grabs my hand, and I can see regret in her eyes.

"Grandma Betty fell, but she's fine, and Tobias went to stay with her for a while."

My heart lurches into my throat. Or at least that's what it feels like.

"He … he … she." I can't even get the words out. I spot Griffin across the room, talking to his mother. The sight of him should calm me, but it doesn't. It doesn't do anything. I'm about to have a panic attack, and he isn't the one I need.

"Why didn't he call me? Grandma Betty is my—"

I understand why it isn't here, but a feeling I can't explain washes over me.

He's supposed to be here. He's supposed to be with me at

every big life event. We're supposed to make memories. Tonight won't be right without him. I don't care if it's a stupid dinner.

Nora shakes her head.

"I'm sorry, Natalie. He asked us not to tell you."

"And he just thought I wouldn't notice that he isn't here?"

Despite how upset I am that he didn't tell me, it hurts more to think about him alone and how he must have felt when he heard about Grandma Betty. He needs me.

"I think I need to go—"

"Hey, guys," Griffin says, walking up to our group. He puts his arm around me, but I can't look at him. I'm on the verge of tears.

"You all clean up nice," he adds, and Graham stands to shake his hand.

"Congratulations. I don't think I've seen you since the big news came out."

"I've been busy. My job has been more demanding on the West Coast, so I've been traveling more than normal."

"Busy is good."

"It is, especially when—whoa, whoa," Griffin squats to look me in the eye and gently turns me to look at him completely. "What's going on?"

I don't answer him, so he scans the group, but not a single one speaks up.

Griffin grabs my hand and pulls me to a quiet corner of the room.

"Talk to me," he says calmly. "Did something happen to Tobias? I noticed he isn't here."

I nod. "His grandma fell, and he left today to go help her."

"Okay."

"I keep thinking of him going there alone, and I …" The words drift off as more tears fall.

A moment goes by; I'm not sure how long it is before Griffin speaks.

"Natalie, look at me."

I wipe the tears that have escaped and look up at him. He takes a deep breath and grabs my hands.

"Where do you want to be right now? Here with me, celebrating our engagement, or in Lovers with Tobias?"

"It's … complicated."

Before I can stop it, more tears fall.

"I can't let him be alone right now."

"But you can walk out on me at our engagement party. Our party, Natalie. For us."

Those last two words carry a tone I've never heard in his voice.

I step back.

"He needs me."

Griffin steps closer to me with a look in his eye that sets off alarms inside me.

"If you walk out that door, we are finished. Okay. No wedding, no nothing."

"Griffin, that's not fair."

"You know what's not fair? That guy thinking he's better than me, coming to me and saying we need to be friends for your sake, as if he's the better man. Fuck that. You belong to me, not to him."

Oh my god.

Oh my god.

"I …" I start to back up for the door.

From the corner of my eye, I see Nora and the group

getting up as if the building is on fire.

"Don't you dare walk out that door," Griffin calls out behind me.

Before I know it, Hero, Beck, Simon, Zane, and Graham are all standing between me and Griffin.

"I'd stop right there if I were you," Hero says quietly but with authority.

"This is a conversation between me and my fiancée. Why don't you all go back to your table and—"

"Let's go," I say and turn. Nora hands me my purse.

"Get back here," Griffin yells. "Nikki!"

My back stiffens, and I stop for the briefest of moments to look over my shoulder.

"Natalie, I meant Natalie."

"Go to hell, Griffin," I say and march right out the door with my friends at my side.

"What just happened?" Nora says, looping her arm with mine.

"Griffin and I just broke up."

"Oh my god. Are you okay?" Calla asks.

"Yes. I just need someone to take me to my car."

"Why not home?"

"Because."

"Because why?" Hero asks.

"Because I need to go to Lovers."

"This is the best day ever," Beck says.

"Beckett!" Calla smacks him in the back of the head.

His gaze snaps to mine. "Worst day. Worst day ever, I mean. I'm too caught up in the excitement to think straight."

"We can drive you," Simon says, placing his hand on

Greer's lower back and pointing to his truck. "I'm parked the closest."

"Thank you."

"Call me when you get there!" Nora shouts behind me.

I climb into the truck and pull my phone from my purse. Not a single missed call or text from him.

As soon as I find out Grandma Betty is okay and I see it for myself, I'm going to give Tobias a piece of my mind.

CHAPTER NINE
TOBIAS

I shut my phone off after about the hundredth text notification.

In my mind, it's either the guys texting me about the party or one of them caved under Natalie's pressure and told her what happened, where I am, and she's madder than hell at me.

What's more than madder than hell?

I don't know.

Right now, both sound like options I don't want.

I let out a sigh, leaning back in the chair beside Grandma Betty's hospital bed and glancing up at the clock.

It's almost ten, and chances are, Grandma isn't going to wake up again until morning. I knew that as soon as she fell asleep a couple of hours ago, but still, I wanted to sit here just in case.

All in all, no broken bones, but she's pretty banged up, so they decided to keep her overnight at the hospital. She bruises worse than she used to, and although she says she's okay, I worry. I don't want her staying home alone right now.

I knew as soon as her neighbor and I hung up that I'd be staying with her until I could figure something out.

I should go to her house and get her things moved down to the main floor guest room. Her right leg is going to be sore for a while, and stairs clearly aren't her thing right now. I should probably start looking for a house here without them. No more taking chances.

I don't care how much she argues—she needs something smaller.

I stand, kiss her forehead, and then head out for the parking garage.

I let out a breath as I drive the short distance to my grandma's house.

Everywhere in Lovers takes less than ten minutes to reach. It's the perfect small town for her. The only time it's busy is when there's an event at Lovers Lodge about twenty minutes outside of town and during the touristy summer season. There was a time when I thought I'd move here after college, but then I met my friends and, well, things changed.

Now, I'm right back to the moving mindset.

Hell, I can't stay in Wind Valley now and watch Griffin and Natalie live happily ever after, knowing I lost her to him.

Just like he said I would.

I slowly pull into the driveway, glancing at the house next door.

Mike. Mikey, as Grandma called him.

I'm not a violent person, but when he came in and kissed her cheek, I wanted to slug him. I was half out of my chair, too, but Grandma shot me a look like she knew what I was thinking.

He'd brought her a few things from her house and stopped at the small store where they have her favorite cookies.

It's hard to dislike someone who only wants to see her smile.

I'll owe him an apology tomorrow for snapping at him on the phone.

I get out of my truck, basically dragging myself inside to get some rest. I really didn't do much, but hell, worry takes a lot out of you.

Worry for my grandma and for Natalie. How mad is she?

Fuck.

I really don't want to lose her over a stupid fight. I might have fucked up by giving her space. Did that make me look guilty? I know I didn't do anything wrong, but Griffin clearly made it seem like I did.

I change the sheets on my grandma's bed to fresh ones. I'll move her things in the morning before I go back to the hospital.

I shower and then grab my computer, making a spot in bed to get some work done. I intend to clear my mind of this day by writing, but my mind keeps going back to the fact that somehow, in a short period of time, I've managed to lose my career and my best friend.

Grandma Betty would be so disappointed if she knew.

I rub the spot between my eyes and sigh.

I need to call my sister, Quinn, and see where she's at these days and whether her schedule will allow her to come here while I take care of things in Wind Valley. Moving here makes the most sense for me, but I'll need to get some things in order first.

Starting with sleep.

I close my computer and settle into bed.

Tomorrow is going to be crazy.

My eyes are just closed when pounding on the door startles me upright.

What the hell?

The noise resumes, so I jog down the stairs and into the living room.

Who the hell would be beating on the door like this right now?

If it's Mike, he's in for rude awakening. No one comes to my grandma's house like this. Ever.

Instead of peeking out the window, I swing the door open, ready to lay into whoever thinks they can show up this rudely, but nothing comes out.

I swear, my jaw drops as I suck in a breath.

"Holy fuck."

"Is she okay?" Natalie steps through the doorway and wraps her arms around me.

I don't reply right away. I'm too shocked that she's here right now.

I return the hug and then step back and hold her at arm's length.

"Shit, Nat, look at you." I whistle to drive my point home, taking in her off-white skintight dress, the way her makeup and hair make her eyes pop. Nothing about her says she just drove for the last two hours. "You're undeniably stunning. I … I have no other words for you right now. Just let me look at you."

I'm not sure what I expected her to say in reply to that, but I sure as hell didn't expect her to slap my arm.

"Tobias Banks, how dare you not call me before you left town? How dare you keep something that involves Grandma Betty from me? This is not okay."

Tears she had clearly been holding in start to fall, so I pull her to me, cupping the back of her head.

"She's fine, Nat. I can bring her home tomorrow. She's going to be fine. Wait." I crouch and hold her face between my hands to look her in the eyes. "You shouldn't be here. Tonight is your engagement party. You should be there. Not here."

Fuck. Maybe if I hadn't turned my phone off, I could have told her to stay.

"No. This is where I'm supposed to be. I want to go see her in the morning, and I want to be here when you bring her home. I want to help."

"Natalie, you—"

"It's the least you can do after keeping me in the dark. Friends don't do that to each other."

She blows out a breath and then tosses her purse onto the couch and drops to sit next to it.

"You should have called me," she says softly, looking over the back of the couch at me.

I close the door and then take a seat by her.

"I know. I'm sorry."

"I'm sorry too," she says. "I'm so, so sorry."

She scoots closer to me and leans her head onto my shoulder.

She doesn't say anything more, and neither do I.

I have so many questions. Too many, but right now, I feel like I can breathe better than I have in months.

It's just me and Natalie.

If there's anything else we have to talk about, it can wait until the morning.

For now, I just want as much time as she will give me.

80

CHAPTER TEN
NATALIE

The moment I wake up, the last twenty-four hours race through my mind. Guilt, relief, sadness, anger—they all hit me at once.

I roll to my back and look at the plain white ceiling, blowing out a breath.

Did I really walk out on my engagement party, and did my ex-fiancé really call me by another woman's name?

A name his mother always called me.

A name that clearly meant something to them.

Yes, yes it did happen.

I drape my arms over my eyes.

Fuck Griffin.

I can't believe he fooled me as badly as he did. How was I so blind? How did I not notice or look for it?

The fact that Tobias didn't even like him was a sure sign. Tobias likes everyone, but Griffin is different.

I try not to cry at how I'd told myself that Tobias didn't

like him only because he took up Tobias's share of my attention, but turns out, Tobias was onto something.

I hear a noise from the kitchen.

I've been such a shitty friend for the last couple of days. I owe him an apology. A big one.

All thoughts of Griffin and my broken engagement vanish as I run my fingers through my hair and step out of my room to search for Tobias. I tug at the shirt he'd loaned me to wear. It barely touches my knees.

That said, this shirt smells like him, and having his scent surrounding me since the moment I got here last night … it's exactly what I needed.

It's calming having him this close.

Especially now.

I step into the kitchen, and Tobias looks my way instantly.

"Morning." He smiles as he closes the refrigerator. "Did you sleep okay?"

"Mm-hmm, great."

"Good to hear. So, um … ugh, I'll just get right to it and ask: how much more does Griffin hate me?" Tobias whisks some eggs in a bowl.

That's right. He doesn't know that Griffin and I broke up. I was so caught up in getting to him and his reaction at seeing me after our fight that I didn't tell him. Last night there was a lot to take in. Now that my mind has had time to recoup and get rest, now is as good a time as any.

"That bad, huh?" he asks when I don't say anything.

I sigh. "I don't know. Not much more than he could hate me right now, but I don't really care."

It's a weird feeling to not care. Hell, we were together for four years, but how it ended and the way he called me another woman's name sort of released me from something. From the grief of what I lost. Because the way I see it, I didn't lose anything. He did.

"He loves you, Nat. If he's even a little bit mad at you, it'll pass."

"Sure. Sure. But we actually broke up last night when I walked out of the engagement party to come here."

The whisk drops out of his hand into the bowl, the handle clanking against the ceramic.

"Holy shit, Nat."

Tobias sets the bowl down and turns the burner off before he rounds the kitchen island and sits next to me. He scoots his chair close to mine and grabs my hand.

I can't bother to look anywhere but at where our hands are laced together.

"Why didn't you say anything last night?"

I shrug one shoulder and shake my head. "You had a lot going on."

"I never have too much going on for you, Natalie. Never. If you need me, I'm there."

I lean into him, and he wraps his arm around me.

"Fuck. I don't even know what to say right now. How are you? What's going on in your head? Do you want to talk about it? What did he say when you left? If he was dick, I'll drive right back to Wind Valley as soon as Grandma Betty is home safe and kick his ass."

This pulls a laugh out of me.

"You're not a fighter, Tobias." I grab his bicep and squeeze. "But you'd definitely win against anyone, not just Griffin."

I say it as a joke, but the look in his eyes isn't humor.

"Are you sure you're okay?"

I nod. "I feel horrible, Tobias. You tried to warn me, and I was"—here come the tears—"I was awful to you. I said mean things. I … I …"

"You do not have to apologize, Natalie. He was your fiancé, I understand that you had to believe him over me. Yeah, it sucked, but I thought you were happy, and I was going to just leave it at that."

He's too good to me.

"I feel so stupid." I cover my face with my hands.

"You are not stupid. He's an idiot."

"He called me Nikki as I walked out the door and then tried to correct himself."

Tobias has to take a slow and steady breath. "He's an asshole."

I nod with a small smile and then clear my throat. "Was he always like that?"

"He had a lot of people fooled."

"But not you."

"He did at first. I didn't start to notice anything until you were engaged, and he wanted to rush it. I mean, you two were together for four years, and suddenly he's in a hurry. It was odd to me."

All I can seem to do is nod.

"Was I that blind, though?"

"You're not blind. Do not for one second let that guy make you think less of yourself. He's the one who is messed up. Not you."

"Okay," I say softly. I understand what he's saying, but it's hard not to think I played a role in how he acted.

"Well"—Tobias jumps up, and my hands feel cold at the

loss of his touch—"I think this calls for not my protein-packed scrambler as planned but for chocolate chip pancakes with—"

"White chocolate chips," I finish for him.

"Yep. It's been years since we woke up in the same place and had breakfast together. I think we need all the goods."

"All the goods?"

He spins to open the fridge and pulls out a package of round sausage patties. "Nothing beats these babies."

"Oh, your grandma just so happened to have them thawed and ready to go."

"Yes. For your information, we FaceTime breakfast three mornings a week, and on Sundays specifically, she always cooks them. There was no way she wasn't prepared for today."

My heart swells anytime Tobias mentions his relationship with his grandma. I swear, outside of the "I'm a romance writer" line that I thought was a pickup move, the day he told me he was going grocery shopping for his grandma, I swore he was finally hitting on me.

Turns out, he was 100 percent shopping for his grandma. It took only a few more times of Tobias just being Tobias for me to realize that he's, without a doubt, one of the best people I've ever met, and his natural kindness is just that. He was never hitting on me. He's just genuinely a good guy.

If I ever start to doubt that there are any good ones left, I just need to look at Tobias.

And I didn't believe him. Wow. I'm a shitty friend.

Tobias is the best person in my life, and I want him to stay that way forever.

He starts to stir the pancake mix, and my eyes are drawn

to way his arms flex as he stirs the spoon in a circle. I've seen his muscles before, but right now I'm drawn to them.

I can't explain it, but watching him in the kitchen … he looks different.

"Why are you looking at me like that?" he asks.

"Huh." He catches me off guard. "Sorry. I think I zoned out."

He keeps his gaze on me for a moment longer.

"Okay. How many pancakes do you want?" he asks, cutting open the sausage.

"I think this is a two-patty day."

He spins and points the spatula at me.

"Maybe even three."

He returns to cooking, and I blow out a breath and hop off my stool to get my phone in the room I slept in.

Being around Tobias feels different right now.

Maybe it's because yesterday I thought I'd lost him as part of life forever, but now I'm here with him and, despite my life-changing events, I couldn't be happier.

"Hey, Tobias," I say, pausing in the doorway to the kitchen.

"Yeah?"

"Were you going to come last night?"

He turns to look at me.

"Yeah, I was. You're my bestie, Dove. Your big moments are my big moments, remember?"

Dove.

My heart swells at the nickname I haven't heard in years.

I give him a single nod and then head for the guest room.

Truth be told, if there was any place I'd want to be after ending my engagement, with Tobias is the top spot.

I flip my phone over to see my notifications: Nora's texts, missed calls from my parents and sister, about thirty missed calls and even more text messages from Griffin.

I delete them all without listening to the voicemails or reading his texts.

I toss the phone onto the bed and then lean back, cover my eyes, and groan.

"Why is this my life?" I say to no one.

"Because even in our thirties, we're still trying to figure out this thing called life," Tobias says in the doorway.

I jerk and give him a sheepish smile.

"I didn't know you were into eavesdropping now."

"I'm not." He crosses his arms and leans against the doorframe. "I'm into making sure you didn't come in here to cry on your own."

"Oh. I still might."

"Not alone."

Well, hell, comments like that might be what sends me over the edge.

A subject change is very needed for me right now.

"So"—I start and hop to my feet, flicking my hand to the shirt he loaned me last night—"can I raid your sister's stash of clothes now, and what's the plan for today? When can we go get Grandma Betty? I can't wait to see her."

He smirks and then tilts his head behind him. "Food first while it's still warm, and then you can get ready."

"And Grandma Betty?" I ask again.

"Is going to lose her mind when she sees you."

His gaze slowly tracks over my body, and when it gets to the hem of his shirt, he clears his throat and snaps his gaze back to mine. "Let's eat."

We dish up and eat in silence.

He glances at me a few times, and you'd think it would be weird, because I know what he wants to talk about, but it's not.

Nothing with Tobias is ever weird.

"How long are you planning to stay here?" I ask just as I finish clearing my plate.

"I'm not sure. I'm going to call Quinn later and see if she can come for a bit."

I nod slowly.

Griffin and I were living together in his house, so I'm not sure where I'll go or what I should do when I get back.

Ugh. There is so much for me to figure out from here.

"Tobias?"

"Yeah?"

"Can I stay here with you until you go back?"

His lips stretch into a grin.

"I wouldn't have it any other way."

"Okay. Thank you."

"And Natalie?"

"Yeah?"

"When we get back to Wind Valley, you're moving in with me."

I bite my lip before I smile. "Thank you," I whisper.

He winks and then gets back to his breakfast.

God, I've missed him.

This.

Us.

That's why this is exactly where I need to be right now.

CHAPTER ELEVEN
TOBIAS

Griffin is lucky he's in another town right now.

God. I want to punch him in the face. Right between the eyes. I want to hit him so hard that both eyes swell, and he can't see for weeks.

Fucking bastard.

I let out a breath.

Why am I so angry these days?

Oh, I know. Who does that to a woman like Natalie?

An idiot. That's who.

I might be lost in my own shit, but I don't treat people like garbage. So at least I have that going for me.

I turn the shower off and then swipe my hand over the mirror to clear the steam.

I've got my Dove back.

I should be on cloud nine right now.

Maybe even higher than that. What would that be? Over the moon.

I shake my head and run a towel over my head to dry my hair.

Natalie is here with me.

She's not getting married.

She's not mad at me anymore.

Yeah, the circumstances aren't ideal, but for the first time in a long time, I feel like things are about to get better. Like there is a light ahead, and I'm about to find whatever it is I'm looking for.

Maybe I just needed my best friend back.

Or maybe it's because she looks too good in nothing but my shirt. Sure, she could have worn something of my sister's last night, but it was late, and it was easier to grab my shirt than dig through Quinn's dresser here to find something.

Watching Natalie wear my clothes … I couldn't keep my eyes off her. Especially this morning after she told me the engagement was off.

Shit.

Shit.

My mind shouldn't go there.

It never goes there, so why is it now?

Is she okay? Really okay?

I know I asked her. Maybe a few too many times, but it's as if she isn't even fazed by the fact that a week ago, she was talking about flower arrangements and colors and cake flavors and today she's … not.

"Hey, are we—shoot, sorry," Natalie says and turns around as I step out of the bathroom and quickly lower my towel to cover myself. "Whoa."

Before I can say anything, she erupts into laughter. It does nothing positive for my ego.

"Tobias! Ten years. We made it ten years before one of us walked in and caught the other one naked."

The playful tone in her voice makes me smirk. *There she is. My Natalie.*

"Well, normally we knock on the door before coming in."

"The door was wide open. How was I supposed to know you'd be in here naked? Normal people close the door while they get dressed."

"I'm a little rusty on the roommate part."

"Clearly."

With her facing me again, she blows out a breath. "So, what's the plan for today?"

"I figured we could head over to the hospital and make one from there. I'm not sure what time Grandma is getting out, so I'll probably just hang out there until they give us the go-ahead."

"Sounds good to me. And even though you avoided my question earlier about when we can get her, I'm going with you. You can't stop me."

"I figured as much."

She shuffles on her feet in my doorway as I slide on my jeans.

"I'm dressed now."

She turns slowly, making a poor attempt to not check me out. Even if she did intentionally, I know it wouldn't be like that. It's hard not to look anytime there's a shirtless person in the room, especially when you don't usually see said person shirtless. I wish I could say people have this wonderful self-control, but we are human. It happens.

"There's a new coffee shop on the way to the hospital.

Should we stop to get you something? Grandma Betty said they make pistachio lattes all year round."

She smirks but shakes her head. "I'm more of an at-home coffee girl these days."

"Is that so?"

She nods.

"Since when?"

"Since"—she pauses—"since it's more cost-effective to drink coffee at home?"

"Ha," I say a bit louder than normal to her response. Is she telling me or asking me? "If I recall correctly, in college, you said it didn't matter how much one spends on coffee as long as it's made right and sets the mood for a successful day."

She pins me with a glare. "That was a long, long time ago."

I nod and then find the shirt I'd been looking for and pull it over my head.

"Yeah, it was."

"So, should we take my car?" she changes the subject. "It might be easier for Grandma Betty to get into than your truck."

Natalie has chosen to stand in the doorway through our entire exchange, so when I move toward the door, she backs up into the frame.

I tap her nose and smile, locking my eyes on hers.

"You always were the smarter one," I say and walk out the door, jogging down the steps.

Natalie is right behind me.

"Between the two of us, clearly. I'm not the one who would make bets with their friends where the loser always had to run through campus naked."

I spin to face her, causing her to bump into me and look up. Chest to chest, she smiles up at me.

"I've never lost, now have I? I'd say that makes me smart."

Then I grab my keys and head for the front door.

Natalie slings her purse over her shoulder and follows me.

"I don't know. I could probably name a few more," she teases and unlocks her car. "Should I remind you of them in the car, Casanova?"

I practically growl at her.

I don't need her to remind me of things I did that weren't smart. I know the list of things I did in the past is long.

"Okay, and then when you're done, you can give me the list of reasons why you're friends with someone who makes such poor choices."

She huffs.

"That's easy. It's because you're a nice guy."

I cringe.

A nice guy.

The one thing every man *loves* to hear.

"I told you I was waiting for my grandson to arrive before I made any decisions."

I hear Grandma Betty halfway down the hall to her room.

Natalie lets out a small giggle next to me, and I pinch her side.

"I've missed her," she whispers and then perks up. "Let me go in first."

Now it's my turn to laugh. "Go for it."

Natalie takes a step in front of me, and my heart swells. If anyone cares for Grandma Betty as much as I do, it's Nat.

Not to mention, I'm pretty sure Grandma Betty loves Natalie a little more than me.

It's a punch to the gut, but I don't blame her. I have no doubt that Natalie is going to brighten up her entire day.

As for me, that's a different story. I know exactly what my grandmother is going to say to me.

"Knock, knock," Natalie says and steps into the room.

"Ahhh! Oh, my dear! What are you doing here?"

"Umm, hello." Natalie points around the room. "As if I could sit at home when you need me."

Natalie leans down for a hug, and although my grandma is hugging her back, she's shooting glares my way over Natalie's shoulder. Her eyes have a mix of emotions and questions. All of which I know I'll have to answer before I head back home in a few days.

"Where's your fiancé?" Grandma gets right to it, but then she gasps before Natalie can answer. "Oh gosh, I didn't ruin your party, did I? I already told Tobias that he shouldn't have left to come tend to me. There are doctors here who can do much more than he can."

Natalie sits next to her and grabs her hand.

"I'm actually not getting married anymore."

"What? What happened? Tobias, don't just stand in the doorway with your arms crossed. Why didn't you tell me about this?"

"I didn't know until this morning."

"You drove all night?" Grandma asks, her worried eyes soaking up Natalie's face. "Let's get you a coffee. The new coffee hut serves your favorite all year round."

"I'll get one on the way back."

I shake my head. Of course she will.

"But I actually got here last night. I stayed at your house with Tobias."

"Alone?" Grandma asks, and now it's my turn to shoot her a glare.

I sure as hell hope Grandma can read that "she just called off her engagement" look on my face.

"Yes." Natalie laughs. "I stayed in the spare room, but don't worry, I cleaned it up this morning while Tobias moved some of your things downstairs for you."

"Oh, I have a new room now?"

I nod. "Just for a little bit. We should start looking for a new house. One level."

"How about you two get me out of this bleach box first?"

Natalie's beaming smile is all I need to not argue.

"You got it."

I step out of the room to find her nurse or doctor, but my phone rings before I have the chance. A picture of my little sister, Quinn, with a cake smashed in her face appears on the screen.

"Hey," I answer, finding a quiet spot to sit down.

"Hey! How are you? How's Gran? My phone died, and I just saw your messages."

Quinn's talking a mile a minute, and I can hear noise in the background, as if she's outside on a busy street.

"It's 2024, Quinn. How does anyone's phone die?"

"Stop parenting me and tell me about Gran."

I groan.

"She's doing better. I'm looking for her doctor now to check her out so I can take her home. Where are you?"

"New York. Just for a couple of more days."

"Wow, okay. How is it?"

"Not as glamorous as the first time and still busy as ever, but you know me, I love the go, go, go life."

"You wouldn't be you if not. But hey, do you think you can come stay with Grandma after New York? I can stay until then."

"Of course. Give me a few days, and I'll be there."

"Thank you."

"Yeah, and hey, when does your next book release? I have a new friend who is obsessed with your writing, and I thought I'd send her a signed copy."

I pinch the spot between my eyes.

One problem at a time would be nice.

"I don't know. I haven't exactly finished a book recently."

"What? Why not?"

"I don't know. I have a lot going on."

"Really? Come on, big brother, I know you've got this."

"Well, that's sort of on the back burner now. Grandma Betty is my focus."

"No way. She'd be so mad if she knew you put yourself second to her. You better figure it out. Maybe think of all the ways you like to relax. Get your frustration out. Maybe you need to vent somewhere. Hey, maybe go home alone and lock yourself in a room and scream as loud as you can. It worked for me once."

I laugh at her ramble of advice.

"Thanks, Quinn."

"For what? I'm sure I said nothing that can help you. The only person who has ever been able to help you when it comes to your writing is Natalie. She knows you best, so ask her and do whatever she says."

"She did give me advice, but it's not what I'm looking for."

"What did she say?"

"That we should write a book together."

Quinn squeals. "You so should! I mean, even if you don't publish it, you should do it. It would be so cute."

"Yeah." I scratch the back of my neck and glance back at Grandma Betty's room, where I hear her and Natalie's laughter. "I don't think it will help."

"Why not?"

"It's not what I'm used to."

"Exactly. What you're used to isn't working anymore."

She has a point.

"Okay, I have to go, but think of it this way: You need to get the words and emotions out. Writing is how you vent, so you can do it alone or with someone. It's up to you to choose how to escape this rut you're in."

Escape?

Natalie pokes her head out of the room and waves for me to return.

That's exactly what I need, and I have a feeling Natalie might need it too.

CHAPTER TWELVE
NATALIE

Once, during our last year of college, I saw Tobias in a pair of boxer briefs, but I was so excited about his new book deal that it didn't really faze me when I'd let myself into his house and busted through his bedroom door. Today, though, I'm fazed.

I'm so fazed that each time I look at him, I think of him standing in his bedroom holding nothing but a towel to cover himself.

And that is not how I should see my best friend, not ever, and especially not the day after I called off my engagement.

Grandma Betty and Tobias are both intensely listening to her discharge orders while I pack up a few of the things she had with her when she arrived. We'd brought clean clothes, her favorite green rose earrings, her purse, and a few other things Tobias thought she might want. It didn't matter if she planned to sit at home all day, she always got ready head to toe for the day.

Once everything is in a bag, I grab my purse. I check it for my phone out of habit, but I intentionally left it on the kitchen table at Grandma Betty's house.

I'm sure word has spread by now, and the last thing I want is texts and calls about something I don't want to discuss. I've texted my parents, sister, and the girls about it. That's everyone who needs to know. It's over. End of story.

"Okay, we're all set," Tobias announces just as a nurse helps his grandma into a wheelchair.

"Let's go," she says, twirling her hand in the air.

She might be crazy at times, but she's one of the best souls I've ever met.

I'm not saying that there is a right or wrong question to ask someone when they call off their engagement, but as soon as Tobias left the room earlier, she asked me if I was happy.

It was weird the way I didn't even hesitate to say yes.

I was ready to marry Griffin, but the moment I picked Tobias over him, even before Griffin called me another woman's name, I knew it was over.

Grandma Betty had nodded as if that were the end of the conversation and then tried to get me to spill the beans on Tobias's dating life.

No surprise there. He doesn't have one.

She then went on to say that she can feel like The One is close, but I shook my head. Tobias has never been a big relationship kind of guy, and I don't imagine he's going to start now. He's not old, but if he wanted to settle down, I think he would have by now. Still, I'd never say never. If he falls in love, I hope she likes me.

I stay pretty quiet on the walk to my car.

Griffin never fully believed the two of us were capable of

being just friends. He never said anything negative—he never would—but I could hear it in his voice or see it in his eyes: he always worried about my relationship with Tobias. Now I'm starting to think it was all a facade he put up to distract me from whatever it was he was up to.

God, I feel so stupid.

Four years.

Four years that I will never get back.

Tobias looks back over his shoulder as we reach the parking lot. "Are you okay?"

"Yes," I say and speed up to fall into step with him. "I'm just over here thinking about how excited I am to have you back in my life full-time."

"Hmm," he says, and his grandma makes a clicking noise with her tongue.

"Is this how it's going to be with you two?"

"How what's going to be?" Tobias asks.

"It's like you're new friends all over again and don't know how to act."

"Um, I don't agree," Tobias replies quickly.

"Neither do I."

"Oh really? I remember a time when I couldn't get the two of you to stop talking."

"Yeah, me too, but we're older now. More mature."

I swat Tobias's bicep at his baloney answer and laugh.

"Yeah, older, which means you don't have much time left to make stupid decisions. If you ask me, this is the perfect time for you two to finally—"

"And here's the car!" Tobias cuts her off.

I open the back seat to put the bags away.

Tobias is kneeling in front of Grandma Betty, whispering as I close the door.

"Hey, no secrets," I tease.

"Exactly." Grandma Betty huffs.

"Let's get home," Tobias says with a shake of his head, then he helps her into the car.

The car ride isn't much different: Tobias and his grandma bicker, lots of laughter, and I love every moment of it.

* * *

I sip my latte and sigh into the couch.

This is heaven.

I know it's stupid, but when Tobias asked me about stopping for a coffee, I gave him my auto-response. But I only drank coffee from home because Griffin did. He made great points about how much money it could save, so I changed my ways.

It had made me a bit sad because I love stopping for coffee. It shouldn't matter what anyone else believes. I love it. So that means there is nothing wrong with it.

I hear Tobias grumble something from the kitchen as the oven drawer pops to a close.

"Do you want help?" I call out.

"No."

Another clatter of dishes as he shouts *fuck* for the tenth time.

I decide to take pity on him, despite the fact he doesn't want my help, and head into the kitchen.

I take a seat at the table and cross my legs, propping my chin into my hands like I always do.

"You never were a good cook."

He spins quickly and points the spatula at me. "I made you breakfast, and I'm pretty sure you moaned at how delicious it was."

I snap my fingers and then move toward him, taking the spatula.

"Okay, correction, you were never good at baking."

I stir the brownie mix as he leans his hip on the counter next to me.

"You're not wrong about that."

"And yet here you are."

He nods.

"Brownies make things better—or well, that's been her motto since I was a kid."

He nods toward the downstairs guest room where Grandma Betty is napping.

As soon as we got back from the hospital, her neighbor was here to greet her with flowers, and they shooed us away for about a half hour before he left, and she stated that she needed a nap.

We may have been home only about an hour, but Tobias hasn't stopped moving. He's cleaned, moved pictures, moved dishes, and anything else you can think of. He wants everything within reach for his grandmother, to the point that she won't need to stand on the tips of her toes for anything. And now he's making her brownies.

"When I'm old, I hope my grandson or granddaughter takes care of me as much as you do her."

"They will," he says with a wink.

I smile for a moment and then add, "If I ever actually get married."

"You will," he says with another wink. Only this time, his eyes lock on mine for another moment.

I inhale a breath under his gaze but step back. "Did you spray the dish with cooking spray yet?"

He nods once and points to where the can is sitting behind me.

I grab the glass, and together we pour the mix in.

"Soooo," Tobias starts, and I groan. He's about to start a conversation that makes him uncomfortable.

"Why do I get the feeling I won't like where your mind is going?"

"Because I'm about to ask you about Griffin."

I blow out a breath.

"It was bound to happen."

"I just want to make sure you're really okay."

"I am. Or I will be. My head isn't in the best place." I set the timer on the oven, and then I turn to him. He's leaning over the sink, washing his hands. "I keep thinking about how I missed the signs."

"Nat, you can't think like that."

"I know. I know. It's just hard not to. I mean, did I do something wrong? Was I too boring? Was I not enough? It sucks that I'll never know why he needed someone else. Even if I did know, I'm not sure the answer would help."

"I don't imagine it would."

"And it's not like I can ask him. If I have it my way, I'll never see him again, but I also want to get these thoughts out of my head and move on sooner rather than later."

Tobias is just watching me.

"What? Say something."

He shrugs. "I don't have much to say. He's an idiot, and

you're perfect. I wish I could tell you that you shouldn't think any part of this was your fault, but it's easier said than done."

"It is."

"But I might have a way to help you with it."

"Really." I smirk and cross my arms. "How?"

"By taking you up on your offer to write a book together. I use words as my escape, and although right now they're also the thing causing all my problems, I think doing this with you could help. Hell, it's writing and Natalie Miller. My two favorite things."

I try not to react, but his words cause a frog in my throat. And my eyes are stinging.

Yesterday I was with a boy who would clearly pick anyone but me, and today I'm with a man who wants nothing more than to help me be happy again.

"Do you really mean that?"

He nods.

"You want to write a book with me?"

He nods again.

"Like a good romance with sex and stuff. You'll have to teach me all the naughty words and everything."

He lets out a boisterous laugh. "Are you trying to change my mind before we even get started?"

"No. I'm just making sure you know what you're in for."

"Oh, I know."

"We're close friends, Tobias, but this … this could bring us even closer."

"I'm well aware."

"Like on an intimate level."

The look he casts my way darkens, and my heart starts to race under his gaze.

"It's a risk I'm willing to take," he says, and even though my chest is pounding at the idea of writing with him, of him discovering the way I imagine intimacy, and of finally getting to make this dream come true, I know it's one I'm willing to take too.

CHAPTER THIRTEEN
TOBIAS

"I'm so sad that the two of you are leaving today," Grandma Betty says as Natalie dishes out breakfast.

"Me too," Quinn, who arrived around 1:00 a.m. this morning, says as she pours another cup of coffee. "I just got here, and I haven't seen you in years."

She's talking to Natalie, of course.

"I know. I need to know everything you've been up to. A travel blog is huge, and I still can't believe you have three times the followers your brother has."

"I can." My sister shoots a smug smile my way. "But you are a bestselling author, so that's cool too."

I roll my eyes. They'll never let me live that down, but also, I'm damn proud of my sister for taking what she loves in life and making it her dream career.

I half-ass slug her shoulder. "Thanks sis."

"Anytime."

"What time are you leaving again?" Grandma Betty asks.

"As soon as we're done with breakfast," I answer before

Quinn or Natalie can come up with a reason for us to stay longer. We've been here for three days. In that time, Natalie and I have taken notes after notes of the type of story we want to write. As soon as we get back, we're going to make a routine that lets us write together each night.

The book is about a woman who falls for her sister-in-law's ex-fiancé. It hits that forbidden romance vibe perfectly, and the amount of sneaking around we have will be perfect. It isn't what I typically write, but here we go. Truth be told, I haven't been this eager to start a new book in a while. My most recent flops just felt auto-programmed. I've missed the passion this new one has reminded me of. Natalie's excitement over the entire thing helps a lot too.

"Natalie can stay since you each have your own car," Quinn suggests.

"No. I'll be driving behind her."

"Okay, what are you, her daddy?"

The coffee I'd sipped shoots from my mouth and all over Grandma Betty.

"Oh heavens," she says with a laugh.

Natalie jumps up from the table for a towel while Quinn just shakes her head with her eyes on me.

"Whoa, calm down," Quinn says. "It was a joke."

"I get that."

"We should add the daddy kink to our book," Natalie says as she tosses the towel at me to help Grandma Betty clean up.

"Oh, this book is going to have sex in it?" my sister asks, and I shoot her a glare. "What?" She holds her hands up. "I wasn't sure if that was crossing a line in your friendship."

"It's not," Natalie says before I can. "We can be professionals."

I sip my coffee and smirk at my sister. "Yeah, what she said."

"Okay," Quinn says sarcastically.

"Maybe we should add an annoying little sister too," I suggest, and Natalie just laughs.

Now that she's back in my life more, I'd do anything to see that smile or hear her laugh.

Up until the last few days, I knew that I missed her. That I missed *us*.

But I'm starting to see that it was a whole lot more than I thought.

* * *

As soon as breakfast is over, Natalie and I give our goodbye hugs and then both hit the road, but first, we stop for a pistachio latte.

Once we're on the highway, the speakers in my truck announce an incoming call from Natalie.

"Miss me already, do you?"

"Well, I figure that just because we aren't riding together doesn't mean we can't talk. I mean, who else do you have to talk to?"

I chuckle.

"Well, I could call a few people, I suppose. Or just listen to music."

"Where's the fun in that?"

"There isn't any, I guess."

"Well, I have a few more ideas about this book we're writing."

"Okay." I grin. "Let's hear them."

The other thing I've loved the past few days are her ideas and the fact that, between the two of us, we have a solid book. Hell, Natalie has a naughty sense of humor, and with the sex, the drama, and the humor this book is going to have, she very well may ditch me for another book down the road. She has a gift.

"What if they have a one-night stand and she gets pregnant, but he's so distraught over his broken engagement that he changes his contact information, and she can't reach him to tell him about the baby?"

"That's a pretty big plot change."

"You're right. Save it for book two?"

"Book two." I laugh. "Planning ahead."

"Yes. I've been so wrapped up in this book thing that I haven't had time to think about my real life, and I've loved every minute of it."

I nod, even though she can't see me.

"If you want to talk about it, we can," I offer.

I'll despise Griffin till my dying day, but if Natalie needs to talk, I'm here for her.

"Nope. The only thing I need to figure out at this point is how to get my things."

"What do you mean?"

"Well, I need my computer for work. I need my clothes, shoes, and jewelry. I even want the stupid blender set I bought that I hardly ever use unless I'm making cookies, but I'm waiting till Griffin is out of town again. He'll be back in California by the weekend. We still have a shared schedule on my phone. I'll go get my things then."

Ah.

"I'll go with you if you want," I offer.

"In two days," she repeats. "I'll definitely let you come with me."

"Great."

"Okay, now can I get back to this book?"

I laugh. Her excitement for something I've done at least fifty times is an excellent reminder that I shouldn't take the good things in my life for granted.

Natalie Miller included.

CHAPTER FOURTEEN
NATALIE

Last night Tobias and I did exactly as we planned and watched TV with takeout. We've planned out a schedule for writing, and in two months' time, I will have finished my very first novel.

Two months.

Wow.

Last week, my two months from now looked a lot different.

I like this version much better.

As soon as Tobias left this morning, I set up his spare laptop and a notebook at his kitchen table, ready to work. Because, of course, despite wanting to write this book, I still have a job I love that requires my attention.

Not five minutes after I've logged into our platform and I'm done updating said schedules, my phone chirps with a new text. It's from Nora and it's in our girls' group thread.

NORA

Should we have lunch soon?

CALLA

Yes, please!

PAIGE

This week? I'm actually still in town. But
you all knew that.

We do. Because she was here for my engagement party.

WILLA

I'm free in an hour and a half.

NATALIE

Lunch sounds good. I can make that work.

CALLA

Me too!

PAIGE

I'm in.

GREER

Works for me!

NORA

I'll be there!

Listen, I love my girls. I also know this lunch will turn into
questions. Of course, it'll be quiet at first because they all
respect me, but Calla will budge first and start the line of fire.

I get to work, making sure sign-ups are open and graphics are still on schedule for social blasts and a few other random tasks before I head to lunch. Where, hopefully, it'll be the last time I talk about Griffin to anyone.

I'm ready to move on.

It's crazy to feel this so soon.

* * *

About a month into my last semester of college, Nora, Tobias, Hero, Graham, Simon, Zane, Beck, and I met for lunch. It was your average Tuesday, and we simply went to Plum's Diner. It was nothing fancy, but that afternoon will always stand out to me.

Tobias had texted everyone with the invite, and everyone said they could come. I knew that day would be one of the last when our group could just drop everything to get together. So I told myself I would make it a point to make sure we met frequently to hold that bond.

But right now, as the girls come in one by one, I realize that I didn't keep my word to myself.

A lot of what I wanted changed over the last few years, and I'm starting to think I was blind to it because I wanted what I had with Griffin to mean more than it did.

I changed for him. That much is clear.

And it wasn't for the good.

But at what point in life did I decide to stop being who I wanted to be and become what he wanted?

I don't even know how I got there.

The past five days with Tobias have made me feel more like me than ever before, and now I'm meeting the girls for lunch. So what if it was an hour's notice? This is living that life I always said I would. I need to fight for this and find a way to keep it.

My life. On my terms.

I should make the heroine in this book stronger. Use my own feelings to really get into her feelings.

"So, then I told him to just do me right there on the table again."

My attention snaps to Calla.

"Ah, there she is." Willa laughs and shakes her head. "We were wondering when you'd zone back into the group."

"Sorry. My mind is just all over the place."

"Understandable," Nora says. "Do you want to talk about it?"

"There isn't much to talk about. The wedding is off, Griffin was cheating on me, I'm over it, and now I'm living with Tobias. Life is good."

And it's the truth. Do I wonder why Griffin did it? Sure I do. Any girl would think about it. A part of me thinks maybe there is more I could have done or said to keep him interested, been more fun, but the other half says I didn't do anything, and he's just stupid. I like the latter half more. I try to keep her around whenever the self-doubt hits.

"Talk about the shortest short version," Calla says, grabbing a French fry off the plate in front of us. I was so much in my own world that I didn't even know they'd ordered food or that it had already arrived. But cheese fries hit just right.

"Can we at least say what an idiot Griffin is?" Nora asks. "I feel like we can't say it enough."

"So do you think this means you and Tobias can stop

pretending you don't have feelings for each other and do something about it?"

That French fry I was just loving gets caught in my throat.

Willa hits my back. "Calla, slow down. Her wedding hasn't even been off a week yet."

"I know, but we're all thinking about it, and Natalie just said she was over it."

"That doesn't mean she's ready to date yet," Nora says.

"Especially Tobias," Paige adds with a laugh.

"Honestly, I'm surprised someone hasn't said something sooner," I say and chew my next fry successfully.

"See, even she knows."

"But I hate to break it to you. Tobias and I are not going to be more than friends. Well, unless you call co-writers more that friends."

Nora squeals. "You're going to write a book. Like actually, finally, do it?"

I nod. "I am."

"It's about damn time." Willa beams a smile at me.

Calla is grinning too.

"What's with the smiles?" I ask hesitantly.

"I just … I can't speak for all of us, but you look much happier than you have in months. It makes me happy for you but sad I didn't notice sooner."

"Don't be sad. Sometimes something bad has to happen in order for the good to make itself known." I grab my phone and type that thought into the notes app for this book.

"So, you're living with Tobias and writing a book with him? Then what?"

I shrug. "I'll probably look for an apartment at some point."

"If he lets you," Calla says quietly.

"Calla, stop," Nora scolds.

She tosses her hands up. "Fine, but when it happens, I'll be the first to say I told you so."

"You'll be waiting a long time, I'm afraid."

Calla makes a gesture as if she's locking her lips.

"What kind of book are you going to write?" Greer asks.

I fill them in on what we have so far, and Paige raises her hand.

"Yes, Paige?"

"What happens when you write a hot scene, and it gets you both in the mood?"

First, his sister makes a comment, and now these girls. Of course, this topic would be mentioned again. "We're both adults who can handle—"

Calla chuckles.

"Okay, look, I doubt that's going to happen."

Then I sip my drink, because, shit, what if it does?

CHAPTER FIFTEEN
TOBIAS

The Space is quiet tonight.

Too quiet for a group who seemed eager to get here.

My fingers are still dancing across the keyboard as I glance up at my friends. We're sitting at our favorite table, and everyone has their heads down focused on a computer.

The fact that none of them have asked me a single question since I got back from Lovers is suspicious as hell. Especially considering that I left in a hurry, ditched my best friend's party, and then she walked out of the party. They all knew she drove straight to Lovers.

Oh hell, this is probably why when I asked to move today's writing session from Wednesday this week to Thursday, they were eager to agree.

They want details.

Yeah … something is up.

I stop typing, sit back, and cross my arms. One by one, they follow, all eyes on me.

I raise a brow in challenge, but still, no one breaks.

If they think I'm going to be the one to start this conversation, they're insane.

Beck clears his throat and nudges Simon. Simon nudges him right back.

"For fuck's sake," Hero says and shakes his head. "Tell us what happened in Lovers. How is Natalie? Nora said she's staying with you. Is that right?"

"Yeah, thanks for calling me yesterday on your drive back," Simon says, and there is no missing the sarcasm in his tone. "I wanted to talk about the idea I have for the apartment in Colorado."

Shit, I forgot about that.

"You know information and didn't share it?" Beck snaps.

Zane holds up a finger. "Technically, we all knew she was staying with him when Hero told us she wasn't staying with him and Nora. I mean, come on, where else would she go?"

I was ready for "it's your chance" or "you have to ask her out" kind of interrogating—that's their default whenever Natalie and I are single at the same time—but the fact that they're worried about Natalie more than me making a move on her is sweet.

"She's doing okay."

"Just okay?" Simon asks.

I nod. "Yep. She's okay. She just needs time. She's staying at my place for now, and we also decided to write together since I haven't finished a book in two years."

May as well tell them everything.

"What?"

"Are you serious?"

"No shit?"

"That's a lot of information to take in at one time." Hero

rubs the spot between his eyes. "We'll circle back to the book thing, but let's talk about Natalie first."

"Are you making sure she's stocked with ice cream and flowers and all the stuff that cheers girls up over heartbreak?" Beck asks. Everyone looks at him.

"Is she heartbroken though?" Zane asks. "She just called off her engagement with a guy who was cheating on her. Even if she's content with it because he's a scumbag, a part of her has to be heartbroken," Graham says.

I let his words soak in. He has a point, but anytime I'm around Natalie, she seems fine. Really. Like the old Natalie is back.

Doesn't that mean she's not heartbroken?

"Oh no, he's thinking about it. What happened? Are you not making her feel at home?"

"Oh, fuck off. She's more at home at my house than anywhere else. I was just thinking about how … she doesn't act heartbroken, so maybe she's not."

"Or she's good at hiding it."

"Don't say that to him. His mind will go crazy, and he'll mess this up again."

"Again? He didn't even take the chance to begin with."

"I'm right here," I say and wave.

"We know."

"And I'm not …"

"You are. There is no way I'm letting you not confess your love this time." Beck grabs his hands over his heart.

"Someone get him out of here. I love Natalie, yes, but just as a friend."

"Embrace it," Beck says as if I never said a word. "Falling

in love will be the best damn thing that ever happened to you."

"Maybe so"—I grab my notebook, ready to change the topic—"but not tonight. Not with Natalie. Now, let's write."

"Okay, but first." Beck holds out his arms as if he's going to stop anyone who tries to touch their keyboard. "Aside from what I just said, we're all thinking the other same thing, right?"

I lean back, crossing my arms. "You mean how we all want to punch Griffin in the face until he cries?"

It might sound a slight bit childish or intense but fuck that guy.

Beck nods.

"I'm not a fan of violence, but what a dick," Simon adds.

"Natalie deserves better," Beck adds, and I can feel him staring. I can feel them all staring, *again*.

"And now we get back to work," I say, finally changing the subject successfully.

"And you tell us why you're just now sharing that you haven't finished a book in two years."

Shit. I'd already forgotten I just shared that fact too.

I tell them everything. Graham is the first to speak up.

"I think writing a book with Natalie is genius."

The guys all nod, and then we all get back at it.

"And then they will fall in love," Beck adds quickly, and everyone grumbles some sort of an agreement.

It's almost comical how much they're still wishing Natalie and I will end up together.

Me and Natalie. I let the thought cross my mind briefly.

The thing is, though, I just got my best friend back.

Hitting on her or doing anything to risk losing her the way I almost did before is out of the question.

Period.

* * *

"Honey, I'm home," I jokingly shout as soon as I walk through the door that's connected to the garage.

"I'm in here!" Natalie shouts. I follow her voice to my office and find her moving furniture around in nothing but one of my oversized shirts. We have yet to get her things from Griffin's house, and she refused to take some of my sister's things from Lovers.

She's pushing on my desk, and as she leans forward, the hem of my shirt inches higher up the back of her thighs. She's on the tips of her toes, bent over in just the right spot.

Until this moment, I'd never imagined having her over my desk like this. With me behind her. My hands bracing her at the hips as I slide myself against her. Her skin soft and warm under the touch of my fingers.

Fuck. I'll never be able to walk in here and not picture this now. Writing won't be the same. Nothing in here will be the same.

I glance at the ceiling and count to twenty, because I refuse to let myself grow hard from something as simple as her bare legs.

But fuck.

It's hard.

Mentally and physically.

I silently curse my friends for continuously putting the

idea of me and Natalie into my head. It seems this time might have stuck more than the others.

"What are you doing?" I finally manage to ask.

She stops what she's doing and spins. "Well, I had lunch with the girls today, and it got me to thinking of an efficient way to write together. So I ordered a new desk."

"What's wrong with this one?" I ask with a chuckle.

"Oh, nothing. The new one is for me. I figure if I move this one to that corner"—she points to the center left of the window—"then I can put my new one in that corner." This time, she points to the right of the window.

I cross my arms and lean against the doorframe. I know we talked in Lovers, and I should let her take the lead on her feelings because she knows them better than anyone else, but this could be a good time to ask her how she's coping now that she's had more time to process everything. Her feelings today could be vastly different from two days ago. Then again, the vibes she's giving me right now say she's happy, and I'm not about to take that from her with questions about her cheating ex.

"So, what happens to the bookshelf that's currently placed where your future desk sits?" is what I go with instead.

"I'm not sure yet. But we move it. Or I move it because this was my idea."

I try hard not to smile when she goes back to attempting to push my desk into the corner she planned. She grunts again, and my dick twitches for the second time, so I move to help her.

"What else did you buy?"

She laughs.

"Nat, what did you buy?"

"Not too much, and I realize that I should have asked you first since this is your house, but I don't know, it felt right to just order them."

She straightens and faces me. "Did I overstep?"

I push the desk a few more inches and stop.

"No."

"Are you sure? A couple of weeks ago, you were living the bachelor life, and now you have this girl following you around to your grandma's and taking over your house."

"I'm sure. There isn't anything you could do that would ever be overstepping when it comes to my life."

She starts taking books off the corner shelf, and I try not to laugh. Okay, so tonight we're rearranging my office to be our office. I like it.

"Yeah, until you try to bring someone home."

"What?" I ask.

"When you bring a girl home," she says simply, not looking at me and shrugging. "I can be quiet if you need me to be. Or just call me ahead of time, and I can go to Nora's for the night. I don't want to impose on your bachelor ways. Not that you're a total bachelor, but you don't want to settle down. I get it. You like fun and no strings and—"

"Natalie." I cut her off before she can say anything else.

"Yeah?" She bites her lip. "That did it, huh? I overstepped."

"No, but I'm confused as hell as to why you're rambling, and the things you're saying are—"

"Things we never talk about, I know. I'm sorry."

She closes her eyes and waves a hand in front of her face. "It won't happen again."

I step closer and reach up to cup her cheek.

"Open your eyes, Natalie."

They snap open, and the glaze coating them feels like a punch to the heart.

"There is nothing, and I mean nothing, you can't talk to me about."

"Okay," she says in a breath.

Her lips part as she inhales, and her gaze flicks to my mouth.

The thought of kissing her consumes me. My palms start to sweat, and my heart pounds like I'm about to jump out of an airplane.

I want to do more than just kiss her. I want to run my hands through her hair and discover the sounds she makes when I pull her toward me and press my body to hers.

Damn it, Beck. Why did you have to put this in my mind right before I came home to her? She just broke off an engagement for crying out loud.

"And for the record, I won't be bringing anyone back to the house. That's not really my style."

"Oh."

I hold her gaze a moment longer before she says, "So, if you come home late one night, don't worry because you're out having fun and—"

"I won't be bringing anyone back, and I won't be staying out late. Is that clear?"

She nods.

"Is it?" I ask, trying not to let myself get too worked up at the way she's biting her lower lip.

How can one simple action spark so much inside of me?

I step back and sit on the edge of the desk to rein myself in. My eyes slowly take her in again. They start at her face, taking in her doe eyes, tiny nose, luscious pink lips, and move down to her thighs, her bare feet, and back to her face.

She swallows and then steps one leg over the other as she adjusts her stance.

"To be clearer," I say, "I'm not a player or bachelor or whatever you've been viewing me as. I'm a one-woman kind of guy."

"But for as long as I've known you, I've never seen you date anyone for more than a single night."

I nod. "So?"

"So, were you dating while I was with Griffin, and I never noticed?"

God, I hate the sound of his name. I'd die a happy man if she never repeated it.

"No, I wasn't. I've been waiting for the right woman."

The doorbell rings and jump-starts her into action.

"That must be the pizza. I'll get it."

I move faster than her and cut her off at the door.

"Not wearing that, you won't."

She huffs, and the tension that had been building clearly dissolves. She pins me with a glare.

"What's wrong with what I'm wearing? I'm not showing anything."

"You're showing more than enough."

I turn to leave, but she stops me.

"Hey, Tobias."

"Yeah?" I glance over my shoulder.

"Do you think we'll ever find our happily ever after?"

I smirk and wink.

"Yeah, I think we will."

CHAPTER SIXTEEN
NATALIE

Saturday finally rolls around, and I can't believe it's been only a week since the wedding was called off. So much in my life has changed in a short amount of time.

The familiar scent of the life I was living consumes me as soon as we step into Griffin's house. I used to think this smell made me miss him. Now I want to vomit.

Tobias follows me inside. I know we aren't doing anything wrong, but it still feels like I'm not supposed to be here anymore.

"Should we have brought my truck? I didn't even think to ask if you needed to move any furniture," he asks.

"I don't. I sold all my stuff when I moved in here. Griffin already had the place furnished, and the only things we bought were a bigger bed and an additional tall dresser to the set he already had. I don't see any reason why I need them. I just want my clothes and a few other easy packable items. Nothing else."

Tobias nods, then follows me up the stairs to the master

bedroom. We brought one of his suitcases to help move my things. I never got into decorating this house or buying much to make it feel like my own. I should have recognized that as a sign. Or maybe I'm just overthinking it now.

Neither of us says much as I show him which drawers are mine and then start pulling hangers out from the closet. I'd cut a hole in a few trash bags to move them. It all feels weird, but it needs to be done.

The funny thing is, I'm more excited to move in with Tobias than I was the day that I moved in with Griffin.

I let out a sigh and sit down on the bed. How did I not see any of this? I was happy, wasn't I?

God, this is so stupid.

I know I was happy. I'm not the one who did something wrong, and I hate that Griffin's choices are making me rethink who I am.

I could scream. It's not fair.

If anything, I'm sad that he wasted four years of my life. I'll never get those back.

Tobias crouches in front of me, one hand cupping my face and gently guiding me to look at him.

"What's going on in that pretty head of yours, Dove?" he asks. "Do you want me to finish for you?"

I shake my head. "No, I just wish I had figured this out sooner. Does it make me a shitty person that I want to get this over with and move on? It's only been a week."

Tobias looks into my eyes, and a grin slowly takes over his lips.

"No, it doesn't. You have been more you in the last few days than you have been in years. Every choice you've made has been the right one. Don't ever feel like you need to feel different for anyone else."

I lean forward, pulling him into a hug. It lasts longer than your typical embrace, and just when I think there's some hidden meaning in the way we hold each other, a throat clears behind us from the bedroom doorway.

Tobias and I both stand quickly. I step toward Griffin, but Tobias moves next to me, half shielding my body from my ex-fiancé. His hands bunch at his sides.

"Griffin, I thought you were in California today," I say.

"There was a change of plans," he says in a clipped tone and crosses his arms. His gaze is on Tobias, and there is nothing friendly about the look in his eye.

After a beat, Griffin points at me, Tobias, and the bed where I'd just been sitting.

"This was going on the whole time we were together, wasn't it?" he fumes, then advances on Tobias. I move in front of him, holding my hands up to push Griffin back if needed.

"No, it wasn't, and you're one to talk. How is *Nikki*?" I snap.

Griffin huffs a laugh. "You can't lie to me, Natalie. I'm not stupid."

Tobias snorts.

I toss my hands up. "Griffin, I'm here packing my things. Just give us ten minutes and we'll be gone."

He laughs in my face. "Oh, you're an *us* now, huh? Tell me again that you two weren't fucking behind my back."

Tobias moves fast to get between me and Griffin.

"If you thought for one minute that Natalie wasn't faithful, you never really knew her. She's the kindest, smartest, most considerate, and selfless person I know. You're the dumbass who couldn't see it and lost the best thing to ever happen to you."

Griffin shakes his head.

"You know damn well I was right about you two, Tobias. Damn, if I'd known she was such a slu—"

I have a good hunch where his next sentence is going, but Tobias's knuckles crack against Griffin's face. Guess he was done listening too.

"Oh my god!"

Griffin groans, crouching over to cup his face, blood instantly dropping from his hands.

I move to check Tobias's hand, but Griffin moves faster, catching Tobias off guard and punching him right between the eyes.

"Ahhh! Stop," I cry out. "Stop."

Tobias stumbles back but rights himself. I can tell he wants to keep this fight going, but he's looking at me for the go-ahead.

I shake my head and then glare at Griffin.

"Go!" I yell at him. "If you had even an ounce of respect for me in the time we were together, you'll leave this room right now."

"Get your shit and get out of my house." Griffin spits blood from his mouth to the carpet and then storms out of the room. "I'll be back in an hour. I suggest you two finish packing and be gone by the time I get back."

"Fine by me," I say.

I rush to Tobias and hold his face. It's swelling fast; he's definitely going to look like a raccoon in the morning. I grab a shirt from my suitcase and hold it up to his nose to stop the bleeding. It's not near the amount I saw gushing down Griffin's face, but my hands are still shaking as I hold the cloth to his face.

"Are you okay? Oh god. Of course you're not. How bad does it hurt?"

I kiss his forehead.

"I'm so sorry."

This is all my fault. I should have come alone. Griffin hates Tobias more than I really knew, and now—

"Do you remember when we were in Lovers," Tobias asks, catching me off guard, "and you said I could win in a fight against Griffin?"

"Yes?"

Where is he going with this?

"That counts, right? I mean, he left us to get your things because he was scared of me, right?"

I let out a laugh. Only he would try to take a moment that was getting me worked up and turn it into something to make me laugh before my mind could get carried away.

"Yeah, that's totally why."

"I thought so too."

CHAPTER SEVENTEEN
TOBIAS

My face hurts.

Bad.

However, had anyone been in Natalie's car on the way back to my house, they would never have known. I saw the way her body shook and the way her gaze glazed over as she stared at nothing. Natalie was quickly getting agitated and was about to blame herself. I couldn't let that happen.

Griffin fucked up. Not her.

So, if anyone asks, I'm fine, and it's not that bad.

But there is a chance I might cry a little when I'm alone later.

I'll probably keep that to myself, though.

I sit on the couch and blow out a breath, listening to her move around the kitchen. I lean my head back, resting it on the sofa.

Despite the pain, it felt good to punch that asshole.

I'm not one to enforce violence, but he earned it.

And now, Natalie is officially done with him and never has to see him again.

"Okay, do you want it wrapped in a paper towel or not?"

I look up just as Natalie rushes out of the kitchen with a sealed bag of ice. She ran inside while I was unloading the suitcases, even though she argued with me about doing anything other than sitting.

I wince when she tries to place it on my nose and then take it from her.

"I told you I was fine."

"I can see it swelling. You should have let me put ice on it while we were there."

"We had things to do, and again, I'm fine."

I didn't want Natalie to have to see Griffin again, and I didn't want to risk punching him a second time.

"So, this doesn't hurt," she says, then jams her finger into the spot between my eyes.

"Ouch! Fuck yeah, that hurts, but I'm still fine." I laugh, placing the ice against my eyes and nose as she stands in front of me with her arms folded and a scowl on her face.

"Why are you looking at me like that?" I ask, my gaze drifting to the blood on her shirt.

My blood.

It was a lot more than I expected. Both of our shirts are ruined.

"Because I don't understand why you have to be so stubborn. You were punched in the face because of me."

Instantly, I shake my head. "You didn't do this, Dove."

"Ugh! And will you ever tell me why you call me that?"

"Nope."

"Tobias." She drops to the seat next to me and lays her

head on my shoulder with a sigh. "Thank you for coming with me."

"You're welcome."

I move the ice back to my eyes and wince. She must feel me because she sits up and grabs it.

"Here, let me help."

"I can do it."

"Just stop arguing with me and let me help."

Her commanding tone catches me off guard.

"Fine."

She leans in farther to gently move the ice pack. I shift to help her, lining up our faces. Her gaze flicks from the ice to my eyes.

She bites her bottom lip for a second.

"Do you think people will ever stop asking us if we're more than friends? Or assuming that we're hiding something?" she asks. Her voice is quiet, as if this is a subject we can't be caught talking about. To be fair, we deny it all the time, but we never actually discuss it.

"Probably not."

"Does it ever … never mind."

Considering the fact that my face feels the way it does because Griffin accused her of cheating with me and it's clearly on her mind, I choose to keep this topic going.

"Never mind what?"

"Nothing."

"Since when have you hesitated to talk to me about something?"

The silence in the room thickens as she swallows. "Because we never talk about this."

I nod slowly.

"No, we don't. We know where we stand, so I guess we never needed to."

"Yet, somehow, it's always a topic of discussion for our friends."

She sits back and sighs.

"What do you mean?"

I know the guys never let me forget, but is that the same for her?

"I mean, the girls already brought it up this week."

"Seriously? Let me guess; Calla?"

Natalie laughs. "Yep."

"Beck did too."

Her laugh deepens, then she says, "Do you ever feel like we should just bang and get it over with? Just so people stop asking. Like, we tried, but it didn't work out. Sorry."

Jesus. Is this how she sees me? Us?

Why does the idea of us just *banging* piss me off?

I shake my head, trying to get a grasp on the words I want to use.

"See, this is why I didn't want to mention it." She moves to get off the couch, but I reach for her and pull her back.

She lands in my lap, just the way I'd planned for her to.

"I want to talk about it. I just wasn't expecting you to say we should bang and get it over with."

The words taste like metal in my mouth, and I don't like them.

"So you don't think about it?"

"To be honest, until that day in my office, no. But I sure as hell think about it now."

"That we should bang and get it over with?" I ask to clarify.

"Ugh, stop saying that. It was a poor choice of words, I get it."

She tries to get up again, but I still don't let her.

This conversation has set my mind reeling. If I had one chance with my best friend, what would I do? How would that play out?

The answer comes to me faster than I expected. My heart beats rapidly at the thought of Natalie and I as more.

"I could never just bang you, Dove."

Her breathing instantly picks up, matching mine, as she looks down at me.

"You are worth so much more to me than that," I confess.

She doesn't tear her eyes from mine. I rest a hand on her bare thigh, my thumb brushing back and forth. She still doesn't look away.

"I'm … I'm going to get you more ice."

Her hand rests on my chest as she pushes herself off me.

I catch her looking at my lips one more time before she walks out of the living room.

I blow out a breath.

Shit.

It all makes sense now.

Why I grew to hate Griffin. Why I've been stuck in life. Why I've been uninspired to finish a book. Everything changed the day she appeared at my grandma's door.

Natalie is why.

Natalie.

I want my best friend to be more than just my friend.

CHAPTER EIGHTEEN
NATALIE

It's safe to say that sleep was nonexistent for me last night. Anytime I closed my eyes, I saw Tobias. Shirtless, grinning Tobias, hovering above me on the couch or his bed or my bed. I'd wake with a jerk and a throbbing I've never felt before between my legs. By the third time I woke because of this same dream, I was throbbing so badly, I almost considered waking him.

I groan and drop my face into my hands.

That's how bad it is—or was. I can't believe I even considered sneaking into his room.

But last night on the couch, there was a moment. Or maybe there wasn't, and I'm overthinking because I'm rusty in this department. For obvious reasons, my judgment of men is rusty.

But this is Tobias. He's not just anyone.

No. No. There was a moment.

Is this what happens when a person calls off their engagement? The lost feeling turns into feelings for the one friend they know they can count on the most. Perhaps this is just some subconscious part of my mind looking for something it was lacking with Griffin?

A knock on my door startles me.

"Nat, are you still in there?"

Shit.

His scratchy morning voice sends a spark of desire right between my legs.

I quickly rise from the bed where I've been working on my computer and answer the door.

"Yes, hi," I smile at him.

I refuse to let my gaze drift down to his bare chest.

All right, it might have slipped a bit.

This is Tobias. He's your best friend. You've been around him thousands of times, shirtless, while he was working out, and it's never fazed you.

Until now.

"Are you coming down for breakfast?"

He eyes me suspiciously. I don't blame him. I've been in the kitchen before him every single morning since I moved in. Even when we were in Lovers.

And then the day after the couch moment happens, I don't show up.

His mind is probably going as crazy as mine is.

"Oh, yes, of course. I was just … going to get ready first. Hit the ground running today. I was going to put on my running clothes. You know, now that I have them."

His eyes narrow—well, as much as they can since the majority of his face is black, blue, and swollen.

"Oh, okay. I was thinking we could get started writing today since we didn't have much time this weekend. I was up late last night writing a couple of chapters I think could be great openings. I thought you could read them and let me know."

Of course. *Of course,* his first thought was about the book we're writing together, not last night. Hell, he went to his room to write while I—never mind.

It's settled.

I'm overthinking.

"Yes. As soon as I get back, we can do that."

"Okay."

"Okay," I repeat awkwardly.

He turns to leave but then turns back.

"Are you avoiding me?" Tobias asks. "Is that why you're still in your room?"

I cross my arms and shake my head.

"No."

He nudges my shoulder. "Come on, Dove, I know you. You're avoiding me."

Again, I just shake my head.

He lets out a long sigh.

"Is it ... did I … say something last night that crossed a line?"

My eyes snap to his, and as soon as I see the worry in them, I let out a breath.

"No. You didn't."

He really didn't, and it's not his fault. It's not his fault that I have been obsessing over his thumb on my leg or the way his eyes focused on my lips for much longer than needed.

"You'd tell me if I did, though, right?"

I nod.

"Okay then. I'll see you when you get back."

"Back from where?"

"Your ... run?"

"Oh." I let out a laugh. "Right, right."

He knocks on the doorframe and then leaves me to it.

You know, to go on that run I'd been planning for today.

* * *

Turns out, running is great for the mind, and boy, is Tobias in for the ideas I have. I don't bother changing when I get back.

"We should start the book with a sex scene," I say confidently, marching to my desk in his office. It showed up yesterday, and luckily, we put it together before going to get my clothes. I still need to set it up for work and whatnot, but my computer is there, and that's all I need to get this book started.

Tobias is removing his glasses and leaning back in his chair.

"And why do you think that?"

I drop into my seat.

"My favorite books start with a bang."

"A bang," he repeats. "You seem to like that word a lot."

"Of course I do; it's going to the book title."

"Is it now?" He grins.

"Yes."

I'm not serious, but the room has quickly transformed into a typical Natalie and Tobias vibe, and I much prefer this one over the one earlier. Plus, if we can't joke about last night, what kind of friends are we, really?

If I could have this banter with someone all day, every day, I would.

"Okay, well, how about I send you the two chapters I

wrote? You can read them and then tell me what you think," he asks.

"Well, how about I write the sex scene I think should happen first, and then we can read each other's work?"

He chuckles. "You're just going to whip one out real fast, are you? As if it were the most natural thing in the world to write about the desire two people have for each other. The heat. The connection."

I nod, ignoring the way his words make me cross my legs, and open up a Word document. "Yep. It's been on my mind since last night."

As soon as I say the words, I glance up. He's watching me, but I can't make out what his expression means. I usually can, but this one is blank.

My palms start to sweat, and my heart beats faster than when I was running.

"I just mean that I thought of an idea last night, and it's been on my mind, and if the level of seduction isn't top-notch, you can just teach me."

Yeah, that totally helped you, Natalie.

"All right" is all he says before returning to his computer.

I pull up a blank document and the one Tobias shared with me, which has all our notes. I read over them quickly. How in the world does a whole book come from this? Like, how do you put it together? We know what we want to happen, but we haven't lined up the events yet, and I think that's why having different opinions on how the story starts. Of course, Tobias does this all the time, so he would know the best route.

"How would you start it? I know I said sex, but you're the expert."

He looks up again and shrugs. "Honestly, I don't want to write this book the way I've written the rest."

"Why not? Those are bestsellers."

"Because that's how I've been writing, and I'm getting nothing done. I want to write a new book as if it's my first, and technically it is, with you. So, any decision we make is going to be together."

I smile, twisting my lips to the side so I don't look too crazy.

"Okay. Are there any words off limits?"

"What do you mean?"

"Like—" I tap my chin. "Do I ease the reader in with talk of my heat and his erection, or do I dive right in and say she wanted his cock inside her pussy as if it were her next breath?"

Again, his blank expression stares back at me.

Is he breathing? Is he uncomfortable? Why do I not know this look?

"Tobias? Did I break you?" I ask on a laugh. Maybe writing a steamy romance together wasn't the smartest idea, but there is no backing out now. I'm making a dream come true, and he's overcoming his writer's block.

We both need this.

He clears his throat and scratches the back of his head.

"I think you write what feels the most natural to you."

"Do I just picture it?"

He nods but doesn't look up. "In a sense, sure. Think of how you feel, what you see, what surprises you, and even the smells surrounding you in that moment."

Like his wintergreen breath last night when I was in his lap.

"All right, what if—"

"Stop talking and write the scene," he says, pointing at my computer.

"Ah, are you going to be this bossy the entire time we write?"

"Do you want me to be?"

I shrug. "Maybe, yeah."

"I can do that."

"Good."

"Natalie?"

"Yes?"

"Please start writing."

I smile and do as I'm told.

An hour later, we have officially switched scenes. His writing is captivating and sucks me in with just the first few lines. As he said, he wrote two scenes. One version has the couple meeting, and neither knows who the other is. The other has them meeting, but the heroine knows exactly who the hero is. She tries to resist him, but he's funny and charming. She falls for him, and they have a one-night stand. Tobias notes in the next scene that she ends up getting pregnant. But surprise, the hero is still getting over his ex and has changed all his contact info so she can't find him to tell him about the baby. Two years later, he shows up in her small town to buy her family's winery.

"I like the version where she knows who he is—it has higher stakes," I say quickly. "And since it's from the hero's point of view, we could use my scene as the second chapter. It could be the one-night stand from the heroine's point of view."

I rest my chin in my hands as I wait for him to respond.

"That could work. The setup is there, and it takes the reader right into the spice, which we want throughout the entire book."

He doesn't look up when he says this, which bothers me. I wanted him to say more about my scene and not just the setup. Hell, it was my first scene. I want to know what he thinks about my writing. Am I any good? Is this all some dream of mine that will stay just a fantasy because my writing sucks?

"That's it?"

He presses his lips into a thin line and nods. "Yeah."

"How was my scene?"

I get up from my desk and move to stand next to him.

The bottom of my document is on his screen, so I know he read it.

"Was it that bad?" I ask, sitting on the edge of his desk and letting my shoulders drop. "I knew it."

"No," he clears his throat. "It's good."

I roll my eyes.

"You're just saying that because I'm clearly sad now. This whole thing was stupid, wasn't it? I'm such an amateur compared to you."

"Don't talk about yourself that way, and no, I'm not just saying that."

"Mm-hmm, sure."

"I'd never lie to you. This scene is great. It's very detailed, and you certainly put the reader in the moment. People are going to love that."

"Really?" I rub a hand under my nose to hide my smile. "Did anything trip you up? Did my word choices make you cringe?"

"Everything flowed beautifully. You have the hands in the right place, the breathing isn't too much, and the verbiage is just right to lock them into the scene. You really hit it off with this one."

I drop my hand and stand, pressing my hands together.

"You really mean that?"

"I do."

I reach around him from behind and hug him tight, jumping and squealing at the same time.

"We're really doing this. We're writing a book. Oh my god." I sit back on his desk. "I'm really doing it."

"You are."

I hug him once more. "Thank you. You really are the *best* best friend a girl could ask for."

Which is something I can't forget. These fleeting feelings I felt for Tobias over the night need to be just that. Fleeting.

Ruining the friendship we've finally gotten back and the new journey we're about to take with this book isn't an option.

CHAPTER NINETEEN
TOBIAS

Write a book with your best friend, they said. Make it steamy, they said. You can write sex together. You're both professionals. You'll get your spark back. Just do it.

Okay, okay, so it was me who said all those things to myself, but hell, I had no idea what I was getting myself into.

Two weeks. Two whole weeks have passed since Natalie and I started writing together.

That's fourteen days in a row where I have pictured the scene she wrote on day one over and over.

Holy shit.

Natalie can write. And an even bigger holy shit, she knows her way around the male body and the bedroom.

You'd think this bodes well for me and us as a writing pair, but it's only caused me to take more cold showers than I normally do.

If writing a book together was supposed to enhance my creativity and imagination, it's working.

Not exactly in the way I hoped, but it's working.

Like right now, I turn the water on and step under my rain-fall showerhead, soaking up the arctic water.

In less than an hour, Natalie and I will be heading back to Lovers for a few days. Not only is it the fall festival, which lasts five full days, but Grandma Betty's birthday also falls during the time we'll be there.

I didn't expect Natalie to come with me, but she wouldn't have it any other way, and despite my newfound feelings for her that I have successfully been pretending aren't there, I wasn't about to argue.

I want every second with her that she's willing to give me.

Just thinking of her smile this morning when I walked into the kitchen makes me hard. I can't remember a time in my life when waking up and walking down the stairs was so exciting. Natalie is the first person I see each day, and it's everything to me.

I grip myself; her smile in my mind and her sex scene playing on repeat.

I dropped to my knees, unzipping his pants, face-to-face with the erection in front of me.

It didn't shock me that he wasn't wearing underwear. It shocked me that he sprang free from the jeans and that my mouth drooled to have him on my tongue. I'd never wanted someone the way I wanted him.

I wanted to lick him and suck him until he fell to the floor, joining me on my knees.

I wanted to own him. Control him.

I gently took him in my hand, gripping with just enough pressure as I leaned forward and licked his tip.

"That's right, baby. Open your mouth and suck."

My hips jerk forward as I imagine Natalie doing this to

me, the warmth of her mouth and her hand sliding up and down my shaft as the other one cupped my balls, squeezing softly.

"Fuck," I say with a sharp breath, my hand moving faster and faster.

I've been guilty of putting things I like into my sex scenes—is that what she's doing? Is this how she wants to be spoken to in the bedroom?

I could picture it. Her on top of me, twirling her hips and obeying my commands to move faster. Harder.

I feel that sensation zing into my spine and rest my other hand on the shower wall to brace myself.

The force of my orgasms lately is enough to do exactly what she's written: bring me to my knees.

No one, and I mean no one, has done that to me before, and now just the thought of Natalie has me ready to break.

I come fast and hard, stroking every last drop out of me, and then clean myself up, regret settling into the pit of my stomach.

Thinking of Natalie this way isn't right, but hell, I've never craved another person the way I've wanted her since that night on the couch.

Was I just fooling myself all these years? Was I in denial?

I dress quickly and brush my teeth.

One thing is for certain. Not once since that night has Natalie hinted that she felt something too.

And that feeling of not knowing what she's thinking kills me inside.

How long after a breakup is it too soon to ask someone what they're thinking? If they think of you? If their body buzzes with electricity when you're near them?

Even if I knew the answers, at what point do I risk losing the best person who has ever come into my life?

* * *

"Oh, yay! You brought Natalie with you." Quinn rushes past me to hug her.

As soon as she pulls back, she looks between me and Natalie and then smirks. "You two look … I don't know. Is something different?"

Natalie laughs and looks up at me, shrugging. "Outside of us being roommates? Nope."

"Not a thing," I add as my sister basically stares right through me. I roll my eyes to hopefully throw her off. "Okay, well, where's Grandma?"

"She's next door with Mike. Calm down."

"Why is she next door?"

My sister pins me with a look that says I need to stop asking questions. I clearly don't get the hint. "Is she … are they …"

"Dating," Natalie adds before I say something I have no doubt I'd regret asking.

"It seems that way. She'll deny it day and night. Now I know where you get it from," Quinn adds and playfully slaps me on the side of the head. "In the meantime, there are brownies."

"Always brownies," Natalie says, following my sister to the kitchen.

"Grandma Betty isn't allowed to date," I say, right behind them.

"Just because you're a curmudgeon who can't commit or

doesn't want to doesn't mean the rest of us need to be like you."

"I can commit," I say in my defense, my gaze flickering to Natalie briefly. She's just watching my sister and me with a smile on her face.

"Really? When and with who?" my sister asks.

"With …" I trail off.

She turns to Natalie. "Have you ever seen him with someone?"

Nat scrunches her nose and shakes her head. "I can't think of anyone," she says.

This is really not a conversation I need Quinn to bring up in front of Natalie, not now that I want her to be more than a friend. She'll never look at me that way if that's what she thinks.

My sister spins and crosses her arms, waiting for me to spar with her. Her look says she isn't going to lose, and to be fair, she probably wouldn't.

But at the same time, maybe I never found someone to commit to because I haven't found the one yet. Or maybe I have found the one and just didn't have a clue.

I have no idea.

This is new territory for me.

Fuck. Either way, I need to change this conversation.

"See, you can't answer." Quinn shrugs at Natalie.

Hell.

I pinch the spot between my eyes.

This is not going well.

"When does Grandma plan to be back? Is she going to the festival tonight?" I ask.

"Of course. The dance studio has something special planned, and Mike is taking her."

"She's not going with us?" I'm about to ask more, but Natalie snickers.

"What?"

"I love how defensive you are with Betty. You'll make someone a very happy girl someday."

"If he could commit."

Jesus.

"Quinn. Stop."

Natalie is full-blown laughing now, and I know it's at my expense. I'd let my sister make fun of me day after day if I got to hear that laugh.

"Let's go put our things away," I say to Natalie and then nod at the stairway. "Quinn, are you on the couch while we're here?"

"What? No."

"Oh, I don't want to put her out," Natalie says quickly.

"She'll be fine."

"Why can't you both stay in your room, Tobias?"

"I could sleep on the couch," Natalie offers. "It's not a problem for me."

"You're not sleeping on the couch," I snap. My sister is still glaring at me with a questioning look, but it quickly morphs into something else.

A sly grin I absolutely do not like appears on her face.

"Oh my god," she says. "Oh my god."

I know the moment she figured it out because her smile is wider than ever before.

"I'm fine sharing a bed if you are," I say to Natalie, ignoring Quinn.

"Yeah, I'm fine with it."

"Okay then."

I walk out of the kitchen, grab our bags, and head upstairs to my room.

I assume the footsteps behind me are Nat's, so I leave the door open.

I'm just setting the bags on the bed when the bedroom door slams shut.

My head snaps up to a wide-eyed Quinn.

There are a lot of things I could say right now, but *shit* is all that comes out of my mouth.

"It happened, didn't it?" she asks.

"What?"

"You figured it out?"

"Figured what out?" I play dumb. Quinn can't keep a secret if her life depends on it, and I'm not about to let her ruin something I don't even know how to start.

Or *if* I should start or not.

"Don't do that. Come on. You like Natalie, and you finally figured it out."

I have two options here: I can keep pretending I have no idea what she's talking about and risk her trying to put me into a situation that makes both Natalie and me uncomfortable, or I can admit it and get this conversation over with.

I'm a grown man who shouldn't be afraid of what his little sister could do to embarrass him, but still, I choose the latter.

"Do not say a word."

"Ahhh!" She cheers and claps and spins.

"Quinn. Stop that. Right now."

"God, look how cute you are." She pushes my shoulder and points at my face. "Are you blushing?"

"What's going on in here?" Nat knocks on the door. "I can hear you cheering from downstairs."

Quinn's lips form an O as she looks at me.

I shake my head.

Little sisters can be such a pain in the ass. Even as adults.

"I got this," Quinn whispers and opens the door before I can object.

"Tobias admitted to loving Gram's new beau."

Like I said, total pain in my ass.

"That's great." Natalie smiles. "Because they're downstairs and ready to go to the festival."

"Fuck," I say, and Quinn laughs on her way out the door.

"Be nice!" she shouts.

Natalie leans against the doorframe, slowly crossing her arms, as I typically do when I'm about to ask a serious question.

I clear my throat, prepared for whatever she's ready to say.

"You do realize this is the first time in our entire friendship we have ever shared a bed, right?"

Oh, trust me, I know.

I nod. "Do you want me to kick her out of her room? I'll do it," I say with a smile.

"I know you would, but no. I'm ready to find out the one and only thing I don't know about you, and the only place I'm going to figure it out is in bed with you."

She pushes off the doorframe and walks toward me.

Oh, hell. What could she be talking about? Sex? Has she really been thinking about me too?

She stops right in front of me and taps my nose.

"Does Tobias Banks snore?"

My heart feels like it drops to my stomach. Am I relieved or bummed?

I let out a chuckle, and she steps back, grinning.

"Oh, that, um, nope. I don't."

"Oh, that?" She mimics me. "What did you think I was talking about?"

"I … honestly, I have no idea."

She smirks again, her eyes slowly looking me up and down. When they return to meet my own, she nods to the door.

"Let's go."

I follow her, my eyes only once drifting to the sway of her perky butt in her jeans before I make it down the stairs to greet Grandma Betty.

If I've learned anything in the last five minutes, it's that when I think of Natalie and me in bed together, snoring is the last thing on my mind.

Maybe I should take that as a sign of where she stands with us.

Friends.

Just friends.

CHAPTER TWENTY

NATALIE

I've always loved Lovers. It's the perfect small town that does all the small-town things. The first time Tobias brought me here was the summer after we met. Grandma Betty had just moved here, and there was a festival happening that took up their entire main street. Mind you, it isn't very big. The population is a few hundred at the most. This town is known for Lovers Lodge. It brings in all the business. The food and the people throughout the rest of the town are what bring people back summer after summer.

Still, the first festival we attended was called the Fourth of July Recovery Festival. Of course, the town had just thrown a huge party for the Fourth, filled with tourists who were staying at the lodge, but the recovery festival was just for the town. Most of the tourists were gone after the holiday.

It's no wonder people love this town.

This week, however, is the fall festival. It happens every September, and tonight is the first of the five nights, and they're kicking the week off with a new event. About a year ago, a dance studio opened up. The woman who opened it used to be a backup dancer for multiple musicians and pop stars. She knows all genres of dancing. From what Grandma Betty has told me, not only do adults love it when they come here for a wedding at the lodge, but families love it because she offers day programs for kids. Parents can drop their kids off for a couple of hours at a time.

If I ever decide to leave Wind Valley, Lovers will be next on my list. It's the kind of place I could see myself raising kids.

Tobias stopped into the local bakery to grab his grandma's favorite cookies, and I opted to wait outside. Now that my mind has drifted to kids, my eyes drift toward Lovers Lodge. It's not right in town, but from the main street, you can see where it sits at the base of the mountain, with the lake behind it.

The first time I came here with Tobias, aside from the festival, we rented jet skis to take on Lovers Lake. I wasn't convinced that a lake at the bottom of a mountain could be warm enough, but boy, was I wrong. Lovers is the little town that has exactly what you need even when you think it won't.

A little girl runs past me, giggling as a little boy chases her.

Kids were just around the corner for me and my life. Maybe only a year or two away, and now ... I don't know when that's going to happen for me or if it ever will.

I scroll online more than I should admit these days, and the number of single adults out there who are my age is high. They don't want to deal with the bullshit of dating, so they prefer to stay single. Is that what's going to happen to me? Did I miss my window, and all the single ones who are left don't want a committed relationship?

"Got them," Tobias says, stepping out into the sunshine and holding up the bag of cookies. "Now maybe I can get back on Grandma Betty's good side."

We fall into step together.

"What made you decide that you don't want to commit to anyone?" I ask out of the blue—well, it was out of the blue for him.

He glances at me but keeps walking.

"I thought we talked about this that day in my office at home. I didn't see the point in committing if it wasn't the right girl."

"But how did you know? How do you know you didn't miss her?"

Our steps slow as we near the festival. It looks like the dance instructor is teaching a choreographed dance, and people are loving it.

I spot Quinn and some guy I don't know. Grandma Betty is right next to them with Mike, and they all seem to be having a good time.

"I know I didn't," Tobias says, pulling me back into our conversation.

"But how do you know?" I repeat.

"I just do. It's a feeling I get."

"A feeling?"

He nods.

"Care to elaborate?"

"Sure. But can I ask why you want to know?"

"I'm trying to figure out at what point in my life I'll know that I'm going to be a bachelorette forever."

"What?" He stops abruptly. "Why would you think that?"

I shrug. "I just feel like that's the direction my life is going, you know. I haven't had a lot of boyfriends, and Griffin especially sucked. I'm just worried that I met *the one* and missed my chance because I wasn't ready or … I don't know. I mean, Griffin cheated on me. Maybe I'm not good enough to settle down with?"

I take a few steps forward, but Tobias stops me, his hand coming to my cheek as he forces me to look at him.

"I'm only going to say this once, Dove, so please do not argue with me. You being you is more than enough. It's everything. If someone doesn't see that, they don't deserve you."

My heart pounds, and my eyes drift to his. He's staring back as if I'm the only one he sees. As if there weren't a whole town behind us dancing to Billy Joel's "We Didn't Start the Fire." It's the same look he gave me that night in his living room—the one I can't get out of my head.

Hell, he's staring at me as if he's about to devour me.

I swallow. I'm pretty sure that I'm staring back, telling him that I'd let him.

"Tobias! Natalie!" Quinn yells, breaking the trance.

He turns first, but I keep looking at him.

I know I've made a lot of excuses to myself in the last couple of weeks. I've been chalking up this whole thing I'm feeling toward him as my mind being crazy after a breakup, but just now, I know I wasn't imagining it.

Tobias wanted me to kiss him. I wanted him to kiss me. It would have happened if his sister hadn't interrupted.

A part of me is relieved because, holy smokes, it would change our friendship, but I think more of me is disappointed.

Kissing Tobias would change everything in my life, and that's the kind of excitement I need right now.

"You remember Hudson Asher, right?" Quinn says as she and the mystery man she was dancing with earlier join us.

"Yes, of course," Tobias says and shakes his hand. "Only the best hockey player to ever come out of Lovers."

Hudson laughs deeply as he returns the hand gesture.

"I'm the only hockey player to come out of Lovers."

"Still the best," Quinn chimes in. "This is Natalie."

Hudson's eyes glide to me, and his smile widens.

"Tobias Banks, I had no idea you were seeing someone. Then again, if my girl looked half as stunning as you, I'd keep her hidden too."

"Oh, we aren't dating," I say a lot quicker than I expected. It's like it came out on autopilot.

Hudson glances at Tobias, who hasn't said a word.

"Oh, my bad, I thought I'd seen … well, anyway, it's good to see you."

"Maybe you can take Natalie out on the dance floor," Quinn says quickly to Hudson. "Or dance *road* would probably be more accurate."

"I'll take her," Tobias says before Hudson has a chance to reply.

Tobias grabs my hand and pulls me toward the dancing. The song changes to something slow, but I don't recognize it.

Tobias spins me, letting his hand land on my hip as he pulls my body flush against his.

We sway to the beat, Tobias's head leaning in close to me.

"Sorry about that," he whispers.

"It's fine, but I'll admit, I've never seen you so … cave-man. Is Hudson someone you need to protect me from?"

I've never seen him act that way. I kind of like it.

"He's the furthest from it. He's one of the best people I know here."

"Okay," I say. My lips part for me to say more, but Grandma Betty approaches us.

"I'm staying at Mike's tonight," she says. "Don't burn my house down."

Tobias's grip on my hand tightens, so I squeeze it back.

"We won't, Grandma Betty," I say, patting his chest with my other hand.

"Have fun," he grits out, and I have to force a closed mouth smile so I don't laugh.

"Will do, sweetheart." She pats his cheek and walks off.

He watches her meet up with Mike, giving him a wave as they walk toward his house.

A squeak escapes me.

"Don't start," Tobias warns, grinning as he looks down at me.

"I wasn't."

"Liar." He pinches my side. I squeal again as my body inches closer to his, the arm he has around me locking me in.

Well, if teasing him gets me this, maybe I need to rethink a few things.

* * *

It's after nine by the time Tobias and I get back to the house. It's not late by any means, but the rest of the town seemed like they were about to pull an all-nighter. Quinn included, because she said not to wait up for her.

Since neither of us is tired, we settle on the couch together with reruns of *Friends*.

Ross has just slapped himself in the face with shaving cream when Tobias's leg brushes against mine.

My heart starts to pound against my ribs.

What is this?

What's happening to me?

Focus on the TV.

A couple of close moments and an almost kiss later, and this is where my mind is.

We've watched hundreds of movies together. We have shared a blanket dozens of times. We've been like this more times than I can count.

My heart shouldn't be beating faster, and I shouldn't be swallowing lumps in my throat, dwelling over what every touch from him means.

But I am.

Oh, I so, *so* am.

"Are you cold?" Tobias asks, pulling the blanket that we're sharing up higher. "You have goose bumps on your arms."

"Fine. Good. Thanks."

His eyes narrow a little as he looks at me. There's a clear question in them that I refuse to acknowledge.

I press a thin smile to my lips and look back at the TV.

"Oh, I almost forgot. I have a surprise for you."

He pulls the blanket off his body and then disappears into the kitchen.

"What kind of surprise?" I ask with a shaky voice.

His head pokes out from around the wall. "Are you sure you're okay?"

"Yes, fine. Good."

His whole body comes into view, and he crosses his arms. "Natalie Miller."

"I'm good. I swear. It's just … I've missed hanging out like this," I say. "The past few weeks have … I've been really happy." It's not a lie per se, but it's very clearly not what I was thinking at this moment or even what's close to being on my mind.

"Yeah, me too." He smirks and disappears again.

Which is good because I clearly need the time to get my shit together.

He's. Your. Best. Friend.

I hear the freezer door open and then a cupboard slam shut, followed by the rattle of the silverware drawer. Then, Tobias walks toward me with a rare smile, one that I usually see only when he's talking to Grandma Betty, and it's one of my favorites from him.

He returns with two mugs with handles and two spoons. A pint of ice cream sits perfectly in each one.

"What is that?" I perk up on the couch and try to peek.

"Ice cream in a mug," he says as if it's the simplest thing in the world.

"Oh my god. I've seen this online but never thought to try it."

"Me too, but I knew you'd love it, so I packed them just in case before we left, and here we are."

"Just in case we needed ice cream?"

He laughs.

"Or in case we had time to just ourselves. We have both

been busy with our jobs and writing, so I was hoping we would get a downtime moment like this. Just us."

"Just us," I repeat. "I like that."

There is no one like Tobias. This much is true. What if I just give in and the tension I feel between us goes away? Everything goes back to how it was but better because I get to kiss him and touch him all I want.

What if it could be good?

"But what if you ruin it?"

"What?" Tobias asks.

"Huh?"

"What if you ruin what?"

Oh, shit. Did I say that part out loud?

"Nothing. What?"

He lets out the biggest groan and sets his ice cream down. I do the same.

I feel like I'm going to be sick waiting for him to speak. Luckily, he doesn't make me wait long.

"This is stupid," he says and puts one hand on my knee. His other hand goes to my cheek.

His touch escalates my heart rate and my breathing at the same time.

"Dove, I want to kiss you. I want to do more than kiss you."

His confession ignites something inside me. My body itches to climb into his lap and do exactly what he wants.

But the dread of how this could end badly pierces my heart and wins.

"I want that too," I say softly, swallowing the lump in my throat and closing my eyes. "But I don't want to lose you more."

When I open them, the chocolate eyes that have seen me and been there for me for the last decade are gazing back.

"What do we do now?" I ask.

He kisses my forehead and then leans back, his arm resting over my shoulders as he holds me close.

"We do nothing," he says. "We just keep being us."

Just keep being us?

He makes it sound so easy, but why do I feel like it isn't?

CHAPTER TWENTY-ONE
TOBIAS

I can't remember the last time I slept on a couch, let alone on a sofa with another person.

Natalie is lying directly on top of me, her head just barely touching my chin as she sleeps soundly.

Fuck.

We almost kissed yesterday. We almost kissed last night. Hell, I told her I wanted to kiss her and more, and she said she wanted that too.

But she's the smart one and reminded me of the consequences. Kissing your best friend doesn't always work out the way you want it to, but every once in a while, it's the perfect match. I wanted to argue that that could be us, but her voice was so soft and full of worry when she said she didn't want to lose me. The reality of our situation came crashing down, and there is no way I can guarantee things will work for us.

Natalie and I will be just friends.

Even as I say it, the words hurt my heart.

This, right here. I look down at her small nose and her

beautiful long, thick lashes. This woman is so much more to me than a friend.

Fuck. What am I going to do?

The front door shuts with a loud bang, followed by a *dammit*.

Natalie stirs, lifting her head as we both look over the side of the couch to see my sister sneaking in, carrying her shoes.

"What the hell, Quinn? Are you just coming home?"

She freezes, eyes wide.

Natalie pushes off me so that we can sit up, but it's cold without her.

Just when I think I have no idea how to navigate the women in my life, Grandma Betty walks in, whistling.

"Morning, kids," she says with a big smile, walking right past us to the kitchen.

Quinn laughs and points. "Oh, sounds like someone—"

"Don't you dare say it," I whisper-shout as Natalie slaps my arms with laughter.

Quinn rolls her eyes and goes up to her room.

"You do know they're both grown women, right?" Natalie asks, pulling the blanket we'd been using to her chin and leaning against my shoulder.

"I do. It doesn't make me worry about them any less."

"Mm," she hums, "You really are one of a kind, aren't you?"

I lean down to kiss the top of her head.

"I am."

But clearly not enough to take a chance on.

"I expect the two of you to be at the bake-off later. I reserved a table for you," Grandma Betty says as I come down the stairs fresh from my shower. Natalie is sitting at the table in a long dusty pink skirt and a black top cropped at the waist.

She's trying to kill me, isn't she?

Her hair is pulled into a loose bun as she listens to my grandmother give us orders.

"I also expect you two to actually sleep in a bed tonight. That couch will destroy your back in the blink of an eye."

"We'll be sure to sleep in the bed tonight," I assure her, finally pulling my gaze off Nat to pour myself a glass of water.

"It starts at one." Grandma Betty points her finger at me. "I expect lots of baked goods when I get home tomorrow morning."

"What? Where are you going?"

"Calm down, sweetheart. I'm just staying with Mike until you kids go home, and do not take that as any hint that I want you to leave earlier than planned."

She hugs me, and as much as I want to grumble again about this Mike thing, I can see he makes her happy, and she deserves it.

"We won't, and lots of baked goods you shall have."

"Edible ones," she adds quickly, making Natalie laugh and again causing me to focus only on her.

I want to walk over there and kiss her and tell her how beautiful she is, but I'm not sure how much would be too much.

"I'll be back later," Grandma Betty says, heading down the hall and out the front door.

I peek through the doorway for Quinn.

"Your sister is meeting friends for lunch," Natalie says.

She crosses her legs, her flowing skirt shifting, revealing a sliver of her legs.

I steal my glance from them to look her in the eyes. "You look beautiful today."

She bites her lip. "Thank you."

Then we just stare at each other; the tension between us is just begging to be broken.

"So—"

"So—"

We both laugh.

"You go first," I say.

She stands and walks toward me, her shirt short enough to show her tiny torso.

I inhale slowly.

"Did we make this weird by what we said last night?" she asks. "Us."

I shake my head. "No."

"Are you sure?"

I nod. "Yep."

"Then why are you acing weird?"

I let out a long sigh. "I don't know. I'm not trying to be, but I can't just turn off—"

"The attraction."

"Yes."

"Me either."

She leans onto the counter next to me. We're side to side, both leaning back, looking anywhere but at each other.

"What if we made rules?" she suggests.

"Rules? Give me an example."

"Okay, um, you can't kiss me on the head anymore."

"What, why?"

"Because it makes me … I like it too much. So, it's not allowed."

I huff. "Then you can't bite your bottom lip in front of me anymore."

"I don't even know that I do that."

"Well, work on it." I push off the counter so I can lean on the table, which is farther away but still lets me face her for this discussion. "What else?" I ask and cross my arms.

She points at me. "That. You can't do that anymore."

I glance down at my crossed ankles and arms and then back up at her.

"What am I doing?"

"Smirking."

I quickly cover my mouth to hide the smirk that wants to escape.

God, she's fucking cute.

"Yeah, okay," I say and move toward her. Staying away is impossible right now. "You can't wear crop tops anymore."

She gasps. "You can't wear jeans."

"You can't wear skirts that show your thighs when you sit down." I touch her skirt as I approach her.

"You can't wear shirts that hug your biceps and make me want to—"

She stops, her eyes staring right at my arms.

"Make you what, Natalie?"

"Nothing." She takes a breath and shakes her head, stepping around me. I turn to ask her where she's headed, but she's quicker than I thought and disappears up the stairs.

I blow out a breath.

Well … good luck to us both.

CHAPTER TWENTY-TWO
NATALIE

The bakery hosting today's bake-off was too small for all those who wanted to join in the fun, so they set up a large tent out front and put up three rows of five tables. There are two people per table, and the cheery energy is contagious.

"Do you know everyone here?" I lean back to ask Tobias. It wasn't exactly a whisper, but the tables are close enough together that I don't want anyone to hear me.

"Most of them, yeah. I've been coming here for ten years. I should know them."

"I've been coming here for that long, too, and I don't."

"I come every other month. You come once or twice a year. It's different."

"Okay, so who is our biggest competition?"

"Planning to win, are you?"

I shrug. "It would be fun. What's the prize?"

"A free box of donuts once a month for a year."

"From there," I say and point at the bakery.

Tobias laughs. "Yes."

"Oh, we have to win now. Have you had her Oreo donut with the crushed cookies in the dough?"

"I have."

"My mouth is watering just thinking of having one."

Tobias pins me with a look I can't decipher, and I smile.

So, he did hear me in the kitchen earlier. That's good. I can't have him looking at me with that smirk and smoldering eye thing—not anymore. I like this new look. Even if I don't know what it means.

"Afternoon beer?" Hudson, the guy from last night, comes up to us. He's got a tray of pints.

"Sure," I say, and Tobias takes one too. "Thank you."

"Of course. Good luck."

He wanders off to the next group, offering more drinks.

"Is that normal?" I ask.

Tobias nods. "He owns the bar next door to the bakery."

"Oh, neat."

"Neat," Tobias repeats the word teasingly. I turn to poke him, but he catches my hand and spins me around. "You have to be faster than that."

"I think your abs broke my finger," I say.

I know I should move out of his hold, but he's got one arm draped across my chest as he holds me against him.

I absorb the moment for a minute longer, but when I'm ready to tell him this should be in our off-limits rules, a commotion erupts at the end of our row.

"I told you not to do that."

"It's not ruining anything. You're overreacting."

"They're here to bake, not drink."

"They can do both. Relax."

"Do not tell me to relax. If you want your own event, take it up with the town next year."

"It's really not that big of a deal, Sadie. Here, do you want one? It could help you relax."

Sadie, I assume since that's what Hudson just called her, rears her head back as if he'd slapped her.

"Gross, no."

"Come on," Hudson says, leaning in. "You know you want it."

"Don't mind them," the lady next to us says, having caught me watching the show. I feel bad that I was staring, but they made it hard not to. "Those two have been at each other's throats since the day they could walk."

"Oh, did they use to be friends or date or something?" I ask.

"Oh no. Never. Hudson is good friends with Sadie's older brother, but Hudson and Sadie have always been—"

"Are we all ready?" Sadie's voice commands us to the front of the tent.

"Ready!" someone shouts, and Sadie smiles.

"Perfect. Let's get baking!"

"That's not how you're supposed to do it," Tobias says, reaching for the dough.

"It's fine." I raise my elbow to make him back off.

"Seriously, let me try."

"Need I remind you of your baking skills, Tobias Banks?"

"We're just mixing the ingredients. I can't mess that up."

"Um, an eggshell in the first batch of cookies you ever made for me begs to differ."

"One time. Once."

"Once is enough."

"Sooooo," the woman, Candy, as she introduced herself, appears next to me again. "How long have you two been together?"

I'm not about to jump the gun with my auto-response like I did last night, but also, after last night, I don't want to offend him either.

"We're just friends," Tobias says calmly.

"Oh, by the amount of flirting you were doing, I just assumed you were a couple."

"No, we're—"

"I told her I wanted to kiss her last night, but she turned me down."

The gasp that comes from my lungs is so loud, the row in front of us turns to look at me.

"Oh really?" Candy asks. "And she said no?"

Tobias nods slowly. "She did. Said she just wants to be friends because she doesn't want to lose me."

"Oh, well, that's sweet."

"It is, and I respect her choice, even if it sucks."

I try to ignore him, tending to the gingersnaps we're supposed to be making.

"Maybe she'll change her mind," Candy goes on.

"Maybe. I think it's my clothes," Tobias says, now soaking up all of Candy's attention.

I roll my eyes but finally start to make headway with the cookies, so I'm still winning.

"Your clothes. Well, that can't be it. You look dashing."

He's milking it now.

"Thanks, Candy. That means a lot."

Candy taps me on the shoulder. "You should think about getting contacts or glasses."

"She should," Tobias adds quickly.

"Remind her about it later. I'm sure she'll change her mind."

"Thank you."

Candy goes back to her table, leaving me with a smirking Tobias.

"You're doing it," I say, refusing to comment on what just happened.

"Doing what?"

"Smirking."

"Sorry."

"Sure."

He helps me switch out the cooking sheets. He bumps my arm, so I bump his back.

"I like that you think I'm funny," he says, and I laugh sarcastically.

"I like that you think I think you're funny."

The gaze that he gave me last night before we started dancing last night is back.

If only I knew how this could end for us, things would be so different right now.

"You're doing it," he says, leaning closer to whisper in my ear.

"Doing what?"

"Biting your lip."

I press my lips together and get back to the cookies.

"Sorry."

"Sure."

He rubs my back just as Hudson returns to engage him in conversation. Which is good because I think I just figured something out.

I want Tobias in a way I've never wanted anyone, and I'm only half terrified. The other half ... she's not sure we should rule it out yet.

CHAPTER TWENTY-THREE
TOBIAS

We spend most of the day outside. The weather is perfect, and the sun is still shining when we decided to call it a day and head back to the house.

I push the door open, holding it for Natalie.

"Today was fun," she says, putting the cookies in the kitchen. "I can't remember just going with the flow in a long time."

After baking, we'd gone for a beer at Hudson's bar, then we watched the afternoon parade, which was just four floats long, and walked home.

There are more events tonight, but I'm not upset that we aren't attending.

As long as I'm with Natalie, I don't really care what I do.

It might not be the healthiest way to think, but today taught me that I'd be the happiest man on earth if we had more days like this. And I'd be even happier if we had more days like today but were more than friends.

The thing is, she said she wants to be friends. How do I convince her to see what I see without crossing a line?

"We should order pizza and get our computers out. I think we need to add something like this festival to the mix. I loved today so much."

She turns to go up the stairs, and like it has all day long, my gaze follows her, soaking in her every move, from the sway of her hips to the way her hair bounces in her messy bun.

I rub a hand over my face.

How did I miss this? How did I not see this sooner? We've been friends for ten years. Ten.

I'm standing in the same spot when she comes back down. She hands me my computer bag and then sets up her computer at one end of the couch. I do the same.

Writing in the middle of the day has never been my thing. It's either a get-it-done first thing in the morning or a late-night thing for me. Any other time, even with the guys, it feels forced. But not right now. Sitting down to do this with Natalie feels good.

I've missed the feeling of joy when it comes to writing.

"Where did we leave off?" I ask.

"I'd just written the scene where they're fighting over the guy she was flirting with."

"And how did you end it? Let me pull it up."

"Um, just read it and tell me if you think we should change it."

I open our shared Google Doc. The scene ends with them shaking hands. Our hero and heroine are agreeing to put the past behind them and move forward as a parenting team.

It fits the storyline, but it's lacking something.

"Hmm," I say and then look at our word count and how far into the book we are: 70 percent of our goal. "I think they should kiss here."

"What? They just agreed to be civil."

"I know, but outside of the opening scene, we've built up enough tension that I think the fight could have more oomph, and he kisses her."

"Just like that?"

"Yeah, it was like they were arguing, and he just couldn't take it anymore. The mere thought of her standing this close to him, feeling the warmth of her body so close, smelling her sweet cinnamon hair and seeing her smile day in and day out gets to him. He wants her. No, he needs her. So yeah, he kisses her."

Natalie doesn't say anything, but her eyes are narrowed as she studies me.

"What?"

"I like that. I like the passion he has for her."

"Well, yeah, she's it for him too. I'll start the next scene. How far should we go?"

Again, she doesn't answer me.

"Hey, are you okay?"

She shakes her head, and the dazed look in her eyes clears as she returns her focus to her computer.

"Huh? Oh, yes."

"So, what do you think?"

"About what?"

"The sex. How far should we go? First base, second? Home run?"

Her stunned expression leaves me shaking my head.

"In the book, Nat."

"Oh! Oh. Wow. I thought you were talking about us."

I bark out a laugh.

"I gathered that."

"I was like, whoa, buddy, we just decided to be friends only, and that's not easy, nor is it exactly what I had in mind, and I think we—"

"Dove," I cut her off.

"Yeah?"

"You're rambling."

"Noted."

We discuss how the next two chapters should go, settling on oral for now, and get to work. We eat pizza and take a break, laughing over the cutest tiny dancers who tried to stay to the beat during the parade but failing and the dads who tried to help them remember the steps. How Hudson's brother teased him about setting up a karaoke machine in the bar and how his singing would bring in more customers than Hudson's singing.

But when I decide to go to bed, Natalie opts to finish her scene before she joins me.

I thought I could sleep easy tonight, but it turns out that not knowing when Natalie is coming up here bothers me. Is she going to pretend to fall asleep on the couch? I even consider pretending that I'm asleep when Natalie walks into the room. It could make things easier for us. I'm pretty sure I'm going to do it, but then I realize how the black moment should go, and I have to get my notes down.

My fingers are still busy at work when Natalie finally wanders into the room.

I glance up, and she smiles.

"You should have come down to wake me up."

I look at the clock on my computer.

"Shit," I say. It's after midnight. "I didn't realize how late it was."

"It's okay. I didn't plan to fall asleep." She gestures to my computer. "What are you working on?"

"Just making notes for the black moment."

Natalie yawns. "Tell me about it tomorrow."

"You got it."

She drags her feet to her bag, digging through it for her pajamas. She grabs what looks like shorts, a shirt, and her bathroom bag.

She disappears into the bathroom, and I let out a breath and shut down my computer.

Shorts and a shirt—okay, I can handle that. I've seen her in that outfit a thousand times.

Fuck. Why did it never cross my mind to wonder what she'd slept in till now?

I blow out another breath.

This is Natalie.

Everything is going to be fine … as soon as I get my shit together.

Once my computer bag is zipped, I slide my sweats off and climb into bed in nothing but my boxer briefs.

I flick the lamp off.

Shit, what if she doesn't want me to sleep in my underwear?

I'm reaching for the light to add more clothes when she steps out of the bathroom.

"Now that I've had that little catnap, I'm not so sure I'll be able to fall back asleep."

Her second yawn that follows makes me laugh.

"I think you'll be fine."

She tosses her things into her bag and then crawls over me to get in on her side.

Crawls. Over. Me.

She could have walked around the bed to her side. But no. She had to move her body over mine.

I close my eyes and count to ten.

Why am I like this?

I've never been this nervous with a girl before.

But this isn't just some girl. It's Natalie.

She gets settled under the sheet, doing this little shimmy thing and pulling the comforter to her neck before she turns to her side and looks at me.

Good. Okay, yes, she's covering herself up. She's hinting that all is a no-go and the "just friends" agreement is still on.

What if I'm overthinking all this? What if she's totally fine with just being friends, and I'm the only one with this new buildup of tension because we know we like each other but are doing nothing about it?

"Tobias."

Her soft voice cuts off my rambling thoughts. "Yeah," I say with a slight squeak as I curl onto my side to mimic her position. Our faces are lined up with each other.

She laughs. It's a sleepy laugh, and it might just be my new favorite thing about her.

"Tell me about your notes."

"You're tired," I say, reaching out to tuck a piece of hair behind her ear so I can see her face better. "Get some sleep."

"I can't sleep," she whispers, moving herself closer to me.

My mind focuses on the heat of her skin near mine, how her shorts are barely shorts—yes, I saw them when she got in bed—and how I love every minute of it when her bare leg sneaks out of the covers and brushes mine.

Don't even get me started on the scent of the lotion she clearly applied to her body before going to bed.

What is that, vanilla? Cupcake? It smells fucking delicious.

"Why not?" I ask.

"I'm thinking about this book."

"Yeah? Do you not like it?"

She shakes her head. "No, I like it a lot, and I love that I'm writing it with you."

"So what's the problem?"

"I just …"

"You can tell me."

She looks down for the briefest moment before her gaze collides with mine.

"I just wrote a scene, and I thought of you the entire time."

Fuck.

She bites her lip.

I do my best to breathe casually, but she dropped a bomb on me, and my brain is starting to short circuit. The first place it cut off is my dick, which is very alert now.

Natalie was thinking of me in a sexual way.

"Did you like the words you wrote?" I ask.

She nods. "Too much, I think."

"How so?"

"I wanted to," she takes a breath, "be alone with … you."

"Dove?"

"Yes?"

"Are you aware you're biting your lip?"

"Yes."

I inch closer, closing the small gap and resting my hand on her hip. My thumb rubs small circles against her skin, sending a bolt of heat through my entire body.

"Tobias," she whispers, and I swear it's so quiet in this room that she can hear my heart pounding through my ears.

"Yeah?"

She yawns again and closes her eyes.

"Don't read my words until tomorrow, promise?"

"I promise," I say, smiling. I didn't even think about that, but now I'm curious.

Her breathing evens out quickly, and I know she fell asleep.

I blow out a breath and kiss her forehead before rolling onto my back.

I know we both want to keep our friendship the way it's always been, but the truth is, whether we like it or not, it changed the day she met Griffin, again when they broke up, and even more when we admitted to having feelings for each other.

No matter how hard we try, we won't be the same old Natalie and Tobias anymore.

Maybe it's time I help her see that.

CHAPTER TWENTY-FOUR
NATALIE

Which is worse: saying something you wouldn't normally say when you're drunk or when you're half asleep?

In most cases, I'd say when you're drunk because, wow, you can say a lot of stupid stuff, and even through a slur, it always comes out clear. But in my case, I'm going with when you're half asleep and ready to throw caution to the wind.

I just wrote a scene, and I thought about you the entire time.

Oh god. I think I'm going to be sick.

And I wanted to be alone with you.

Yep, I said that too.

The worst part is, I meant it. All of it. I just didn't plan to have word vomit in the late hours of the night.

The one question I still can't seem to answer is why I said it.

What did I think was going to happen? That one day after we admitted our feelings, on which we both somewhat silently agreed not to act, we'd change our minds and chance ruining ten years of friendship? That I'd say the word, and he'd jump on me because he has no self-control?

Please. This is Tobias.

Every move he makes has been well-thought out. He might be the kind of person to wait until the last minute to make a choice, but that's because he's considered all the angles.

But me?

I clearly do not take that approach.

It's fine. It's totally fine.

"Are you okay today?" Quinn asks as we walk down Lovers's main street to Grandma Betty's house. There are cute boutiques in the middle of town that we both like to frequent when we're here, and today seemed like a good day to do it. Especially since she invited me while Tobias was still in the shower, and I was ready to do anything that wasn't facing him.

I mean, hell, what if he read that scene? Does he like it? Does he think I'm crazy? He's done nothing but compliment my writing style since we started this book, and maybe this is where he cuts me off and tells me that I'm average.

Shit, would that mean I'm average in bed?

"Natalie, hey." Quinn snaps her fingers in front of my face and waves her other hand, which is holding her coffee, high to grab my attention.

"Hi, yes, I'm fine."

"Are you sure?" She pauses on the sidewalk, smiling at an older couple walking past us. "You seem distracted."

Sooooo distracted.

"I'm sorry. I've been thinking about this book so much, I'm struggling to multitask."

"That's right." She beams. "You and Tobias are writing a book together. How's it going? It's bad if you're so stressed."

"No, it's good. He's a great writer, and we seem to have this effortless flow together, but I want it to be good. I've always wanted to write, and I really hope it's helping him too."

"I know. I want him to be out of this funk."

"Me too. He's such a brilliant writer. It might be crazy to think I could write a book with him and bam! problem solved."

We start walking again, and I have to hold my hand up to block the sun since I forgot my sunglasses.

"Honestly, I think having you back in his life has helped on its own."

"What do you mean?" I've always been in his life, so her comment doesn't make sense to me.

"I mean, you're not dating anyone or engaged anymore, so he doesn't have to share you with anyone. You're his safe place. The one he goes to when life is crazy. You're his air in a sense, so writing a book together is perfect."

"I'm his air?" I ask with a laugh. "Have you been reading his books?"

She laughs and nudges me. "I'm serious, Natalie. He's different when you're around. He's happier."

"I like being around him too. Hence, why we're so close."

Last night comes back to me. The things I said to him were not best-friend-approved terminology.

I should rewrite the scene.

But it was so good.

"If this book thing works out, do you think you'll write more?"

"I haven't really thought about it."

"Well, what was your plan for after you got married?"

"Be married, I guess. Griffin had plans, and he added me to it. I just assumed I'd keep working with Nora, and that was that."

"Was that going to make you happy?"

"I wasn't not happy about it."

"Did it make you feel excited?"

"What's with the questions?" I ask. Damn, she keeps firing them at me.

"I'm just making conversation. I've known you as long as my brother has, and it just occurred to me that I never knew your goals in life."

"Oh, well, writing a book and being published is pretty huge up there."

"Then how come you never did it till now?"

I shrug. "I thought about starting one about a year after I met Griffin, but he told me it was hard to make a living off that, and he shared some stuff he read online, and it turned me off it."

His lack of support for something I wanted in life should have been my first red flag.

"So, what made you change your mind this time around?"

Tobias did. The day I mentioned it to him, I knew he might not enjoy the idea of writing a book together, but he'd never talk down to my dreams. He's always been very supportive of what I want to do with my life.

He was even going to walk away from our friendship because he thought I was happy with Griffin. I'm very aware now that he would do anything for me, even if it meant he lost in the end.

Another valid reason these feelings I have for him need to remain just that: feelings.

We change the conversation to Quinn's travel blog and her plans for the next couple of years. She wants to return to Scotland and Paris soon, but being here with her brother and grandma makes her miss her family.

"Our parents are pretty free-spirited and travel plenty on their own, so I'm sure they would be happy to see me go back, but I think Grandma Betty loves having us here. It doesn't matter that she's been sleeping next door; I think she likes having a full house."

"Oh, I couldn't agree more," I say as we reach the sidewalk to the front door. Tobias is waiting, leaning against the doorframe. His gaze makes my skin tingle. I meet his eyes, a feeling of excitement flooding through me. He smirks quickly before licking his lips to hide it.

My heart races, and I take a breath.

He read the scene. I know he did.

"Please tell me you haven't been standing there since we left," Quinn says.

"I haven't."

"So, you just happened to be here when we walk up?"

He only nods, his gaze flicking to his sister for split second before settling back on me.

"Do you want to write today? I have some ideas," he says.

Oh, I bet he does. But also, he's got that smile on his face and his voice is hopeful. Outside of my worry over this scene and last night, the whole purpose of writing together was to help him, so I can't say no. Even if I could, I wouldn't want to.

These feelings between us are trouble.

"Yes, I do want to write today."

"You two have fun," Quinn says, hugging me before disappearing into the house.

"Should we set up in the living room?" I ask, refusing to look into the eyes that now make my body feel like it's about to lose control.

"Is that where you want to write?" he asks.

"I can write anywhere," I tell him.

"I think I need a change of scenery. How do you feel about writing offline today?"

Finally, I glance up. "What does that mean?"

"It means we won't be writing in Google Docs. It'll be a fresh scene, on a Word document, in a place with no service."

"Oh, so legit offline. I thought it was writer lingo I didn't know," I say with a laugh. "Sure. Where are we going?"

"It's a surprise. Let's go." He bounces down the front steps, his woodsy scent drafting by me.

"I need to grab my stuff."

"It's in the truck."

I turn around and cross my arms. "So, I didn't really have an option?"

"Nope." He smirks again.

With my shopping bags in hand, I move toward his truck.

He has ideas, huh? Let's just hope they have nothing to do with the scene I wrote last night. I can talk a big game when Tobias isn't near me, but when he is, all my worries disappear, and for a girl who's not sure what to do with these new feelings, that could be dangerous.

* * *

Almost a half hour later, we're sitting at a picnic table near Lovers Lake. There is a slight breeze, giving me a small chill, but Tobias has planned for this and hands me my sweater and then a blanket.

"I've never written outside before," I say. My gaze floats over our side-by-side screens to the lake that, despite the breeze, looks like glass.

"Simon swears this is the best way to write, and so I give it a try from time to time. I've written some of my best scenes outside, so he might be on to something."

"And what scene are we writing out here today?" I ask, propping one elbow onto the table and resting my face in my hand as I watch him. "Are they doing something outside?"

"Actually, I was thinking of the fight scene we discussed last night and how we wanted more oomph."

Relief floods through me, and I swear I hear birds chirping. He's not talking about *that* scene. He's talking about a safe zone scene that will end with just a kiss.

"Okay, do you want me to rewrite the whole thing?"

"No, just the ending, but let's write it together."

He pulls up the draft of that scene and scrolls about a third of the way through until he shows me where we should start the rewrites.

He goes into detail about the feelings we should include and the fire they need to give the reader, and even though I'm listening, I get sucked into his passion for writing. He really loves this, and I really love watching him talk about it.

"I think he should follow her outside," he says. "And call out her name. The baby is with the grandparents, so we don't have to worry about that angle. We should actually use it to our advantage and give these two the moment they deserve."

"Does she just stop and turn," I ask, "or does she try to keep walking away?"

"I think she keeps walking for a moment and then turns, ready to argue."

I smile. "Let's start with that."

He starts writing, but I stop him when the hero bumps into her from behind.

"I don't think it really works like that. He wouldn't be that close. It seems too easy and unnatural."

"Yeah, he would."

"No, why would he?"

"Because he's following her."

"I know, but that seems like we're forcing the action."

"Stand up. Let's see," he says, rising from the table.

He wants to act out this scene.

No thanks.

I shake my head.

"It's fine; we can leave it the way you have it. You're the expert and know what works."

"Don't just say that to please me. I want to show you how this works."

"It's really not that big of a deal."

"Stand up, Natalie," he says, and my heart hammers at his command, my legs doing as they're told.

I toss up my hands. "Now what?"

"Turn and walk away from me like you're mad at me."

I grin. "I don't know how to fake that."

"Just do it."

I shake my head, feeling silly but also excited. "How fast do I walk?"

"As fast as you want to get away from me."

I narrow my eyes, turn, and then march off with a huff.

I'm about four strides away when he calls out, "Natalie, stop."

His tone ignites something inside me, but I ignore it and count to three before I stop and turn, assuming that's how the heroine in our story would do it.

Tobias is there in my space. His body rushes mine so quickly that I stumble back, only to be steadied on my feet by his hands gripping my waist.

His breathing is fast, as is mine, and our lips are inches apart. His chest is brushed up against my own, and even through our clothes, I swear I feel his heart pounding, the beat matching mine as I wait for whatever happens next.

I don't think this is what we had in mind for our characters, but the move is more realistic than I thought.

I close my eyes and take a deep breath.

"This is a lot closer than we wrote it."

"It is," he agrees. "I like this better."

"So do I."

But neither of us move. "What should happen next?"

"Well," he says in a husky tone, "he should move his hand to her cheek, like this."

His hand cups my face, his thumb brushing under my chin, gently guiding me to look up.

"Their eyes should lock."

I swallow the lump in my throat and nod. "I like that."

"Now it's her turn."

I lay my palm flat on his chest. "She'd touch him here."

"Why?"

"She'd tell herself it was to keep control of the distance, but really it's to see if his heart is beating as fast as hers."

"Is it?"

"It's faster."

"Because he wants her. He craves her."

"And she wants him."

"But they're resisting."

"Yes."

"Why?"

"Because of all the things that could go wrong," I tell him.

"But what about all the things that could go right?"

His words do nothing to slow the beat inside my chest; in fact, they increase it. Are we still talking about the book? My eyes find his to see if I can read them and find the meaning of this moment.

The only thing I see in them is desire, and that's a look I've never seen in his eyes before.

It's one I've never seen anyone give me before.

"Then I think," I start and close my eyes, biting my lower lip, "I think she'd want him to whisper two little words right before he finally kisses her."

"And what are those two words, Dove?"

"Fuck it," I whisper.

Keeping my eyes closed, I wait, praying he repeats after me.

"Fuck it," he says with a growl, and then his lips are on mine, devouring me and stealing my next breath. My arms wrap around his neck while his circle my waist, pulling my body flush to his. His tongue slips into my mouth, dancing with mine as we kiss.

All worries of this moment fade away as I melt in his arms. Our lips move in sync as if this is something we've done many times before. It feels right.

His hands smooth over my hips to my backside and over my butt. He squeezes, drawing a moan out of me that I never knew could happen from a kiss.

He pulls away, resting his forehead against mine. "That was even better than I imagined."

"You imagined it?"

He chuckles.

"After the last two nights, how can you even doubt that I did?"

I shrug. "I don't know. Feelings come and go."

"Don't do that," he says, pressing his lips softly to mine again. "Don't be shy now."

I kiss him back, my fist gripping his shirt to keep him close.

"But we don't do this," I tell him. "We don't kiss."

"I think we should start."

There's no point in trying to hide the giant smile I know is coming.

"You do?"

"Oh, yeah, but we should probably finish this scene first."

He grabs my hand, pulling me back to the table. We both sit for maybe ten seconds before he slams his computer shut, turns to face me with one leg on each side of the bench.

"You know what? Fuck that. I tasted you, and I need more."

His lips are on mine again in an instant, and for the first time ever, I make out with Tobias Banks.

CHAPTER TWENTY-FIVE
TOBIAS

I knew kissing Natalie would change things between us, but I didn't realize how much it would change my way of thinking too.

Am I afraid that we're going to ruin our friendship? No. Not even close.

The moment her lips touched mine, I knew these are the lips I'd kiss for the rest of my life. These are the lips I'll dream about day in and day out.

Friendship was a great place to start, but that's not how we end.

I reach over the middle of my truck and lace her hand with mine. Slowly, she looks up at me with a smile.

"This is crazy."

I grin, my eyes flashing from the road to hers. "Is it?"

"Yes," she says with a laugh. "It is."

Her smile never falters through her words.

"A good crazy, though," she adds.

I nod. "I like good crazy."

I wink at her; she rolls her eyes at me.

"I hate to be this girl right out of the gate, but what does this mean?"

I shrug. "What do you want it to mean?"

She purses her lips for a moment. "Our friends and family are going to freak out, so maybe we should keep this to ourselves until we figure that part out."

For me, I could shout from the rooftops right now that this woman is mine, but as cliché as that sounds, she's clearly not there yet.

I'm okay with that.

A month ago, her life was in a completely different place. I don't want to rush her into anything, even if I already know this is it for me.

It's wild to think that I fought this for so long.

I waited for this moment for ten years. I just didn't know it.

I argued over and over with my friends and family that Natalie and I were just friends and were only ever going to be just friends.

I'm going to look like a fool to them, and I don't even care. I figured it out. What's the saying, better late than never?

I pull into the driveway of my grandmother's house and turn off the truck.

It's going to be impossible not touching Natalie now, but if she doesn't want anyone to know, I have no choice but to do my best.

Neither of us moves. Instead, I rest my head on the back of the seat, slowly turning to look at her. She does the same, and my heart swells.

"What are you thinking?"

She smirks. "That it feels like we're in high school."

"What?" I chuckle. "How?"

She points at the house. "We just got done making out in a field, and now we're at your grandma's house, where we're going to act like there's nothing between us. Knowing you," she says, reaching out to cup my cheek, "you're going to try to sneak kisses here and there and risk getting us caught."

I laugh harder. She's not wrong.

"How would you know that? Have you seen me do that with anyone?"

She shakes her head. "No. I've never seen you with a girl-friend, but you're you and I'm me. It's just a feeling I get."

"It's just a feeling you get, huh?" I rub my chin, never taking my eyes off her.

"Yes, because I know I'll want to do the same thing."

I lean forward to press my lips to hers, but she holds her hand out flat to stop me. She quickly looks out the front window to see if anyone is watching. When the coast is clear, she leans in to meet me halfway.

Both of my hands hold her face as I slip my tongue inside her mouth.

Hell, I've never tasted someone who tastes so sweet. So addicting.

I groan and pull back.

"Maybe we should go somewhere else for a while or tell them we need to go back to Wind Valley."

Natalie laughs deeply and loud, and it's the best thing I've ever heard.

"Now you really make me feel like we're in high school. You can have a little control for one more night. Tomorrow, we'll head back home and, well, I'm not sure what happens then, but inside your house, there will be a lot less for us to hide."

"You always were the smarter one," I say, the way I've said it for years and years.

"I think after the last couple of hours, that statement could be questionable."

"Not a chance." I watch her get out of the truck.

I meet her around the front, and as if my body can't be near her without touching, I reach for her hand. She shoves me off the sidewalk. I almost trip into the grass, but it's worth it because of her laughter.

Will that sound ever get old?

"It's been thirty seconds, Tobias."

"I can't help it," I say as we reach the door. "I have a decade to make up for, and I don't want to waste another moment."

She pauses, her gaze locking on mine. I search her eyes for an inkling of what she's thinking, but I come up with nothing.

Her nose scrunches as she pulls the door open. "Crazy," she says. "Just crazy."

I follow her inside. "But it's a good crazy."

She shakes her head, watching me as she walks backward to the kitchen, where we can hear Grandma Betty and Quinn talking.

Yeah, not touching Natalie is going to take more willpower than my body possesses.

"Oh, good, you're home," Grandma Betty says. She and Quinn are sitting across from each other at the table and look as if they were just engrossed in a serious conversation. Natalie walks to the other side of the kitchen and leans against the counter while I remain in the doorway with my arms crossed.

"What's going on?" I ask.

"I'm leaving tonight," Quinn says and pushes out her bottom lip. "When Natalie and I were talking earlier, it got me thinking. Grandma is better now, and I'm ready to get back to it."

"Where are you going this time?"

"Paris," she says. "I've missed it there, and I just don't feel like me when I stay in one place for too long."

I nod slowly. As much as I believe Grandma should have someone close by for a little while longer, I get it. The whole having a dream and not making it happen—trust me, I get it more than she knows.

I don't say anything, yet all eyes are on me.

It feels weird, and I hate that maybe they were all worried about what I was going to think. Like she needs my permission.

Quinn might be my little sister, who is sometimes annoying and makes me worry with all my heart, but she's also a smart and brave woman who doesn't need my approval.

I push off the door and hug her from behind. "You better eat more of those weird cookie things for me while you're there," I say.

Her shoulders relax.

"You got it," she says and pats my hand.

"And I'm moving in with Mike," Grandma Betty says, standing and grabbing her jacket as if that's the end of the conversation.

She looks me in the eye, daring me to say something.

I only shake my head and look at Natalie.

"Have my gray hairs started to show yet?"

She laughs. "Oh yeah, you have like twenty by now."

"What?"

"Don't worry, though, women are really into the silver fox thing these days."

"Are they?" I ask and step toward her.

She nods with a coy smile and then glances over my shoulder. "Don't you two agree?"

I pause my stride and give Natalie a grin only she can see.

"I mean, not on my brother, but sure," says Quinn on her way out of the room.

Grandma is right behind her.

"Hey, where are you both going?"

"To pack."

"To Mike's."

And then they're both gone, the front door slamming closed.

"Don't," Natalie says and points her finger at me.

"Don't what?"

"Don't take another step forward. We aren't alone in this house right now, and your sister could come downstairs at any moment."

She indeed could, but the chances are small since she just went to her room.

I move toward Natalie, caging her in against the counter.

"We might not be alone right now, but if you didn't just hear, it sounds like we will be very much alone tonight."

She takes a deep breath, her gaze landing on my lips.

I wait just a moment before I add, "And we have a sex scene we need to discuss."

Her smile drops, and her eyes meet mine.

I wink. "You thought I hadn't read it yet, didn't you?"

No answer.

"I did." I push off the counter, walking backward to get my computer from the truck so that I can keep my eyes on her. She still hasn't spoken, so I decide this is as good a time as any to add "twice."

* * *

"Have a good night!" Grandma Betty calls as she walks past the living room with a packed bag.

"You, too, Grandma Betty," Natalie says from the couch where she's sitting with her legs crossed, working on her computer.

"Night."

The moment the door closes, the air in the room shifts.

Quinn left a couple of hours ago, so with Grandma Betty gone, Natalie and I are officially alone.

I grab my computer, get up from my chair, and plant myself right next to Natalie.

She laughs. "Close enough?"

"Not even a little."

She bumps me with her shoulder.

"We need to finish these next couple of chapters tonight," she adds. "It doesn't look like you've written much."

I take a deep breath. I'm beginning to feel that stage in a book where I'm over it, and I hate it. I hate that it's on a book with her. I hate that it's even happening.

I couldn't focus before, and I sure as hell can't focus now. I'm not sure how much to share with Natalie, though. After all, the whole reason she brought this up was to help me.

"Are you stuck?" she asks softly.

I rub my chin. "I don't know."

"Are you starting to feel like you don't want to do this anymore?"

I sigh. "I don't know."

"Are you saying *I don't know* because you're not sure how much you want to share with me?"

"Yes."

She moves her computer off her lap, readjusting herself to sit on her knees facing me.

"How can I help?"

"I—"

"Don't you dare say I don't know. This is why I'm here."

I nod.

"Is it because you're nervous to tell me? Is it something you've never told anyone else?"

I narrow my eyes at her. I don't especially enjoy talking about failing at something, but it impresses me that she knows exactly how to read me.

"Would it help if I told you something embarrassing about myself?" she asks.

"Worse than when you were making out with that guy in government class and farted?" I ask.

She punches me in the arms, and I wince.

"I told you that in confidence. You said you would never repeat it."

"And I didn't until just now."

"That better be true."

"It is."

"But no, this is worse than that."

"Worse than when you ate that ice cream at the fair and—"

"I swear to god, Tobias, do you ever forget anything?"

"Not when it comes to you."

Her expression softens, and she bites her lip.

I reach up to pull it from her teeth, noticing the way her plump pink lip bounces just slightly.

"You should never be embarrassed to tell me anything, Dove. I think very highly of you, and nothing will ever change that."

Her head tilts back with a laugh. "Oh my god!"

Confused by her reaction, I don't say a word. I just let her laugh it out.

"All this time," she says quickly, "you've said lines like that to me for years and years, but now …"

"But now, what?"

"Now those words make my heart race."

"Just your heart?" I ask, grabbing her hips and pulling her slightly until she gets the hint that I want her to sit on my lap.

Painfully slow, she sits up and then rests one leg on each side of me, lowering herself on a breath.

She rests her forehead against mine. "Are you going to kiss me now?" she whispers.

"Is that what you want?" I whisper back.

Instead of answering, she presses her lips to mine.

I guess this means we won't be finishing those chapters tonight.

The kiss starts softly, our lips moving in perfect sync. After a moment, her tongue sweeps into my mouth, tangling with mine as her hips start to move slowly against me. I groan the first time her body rubs on mine, which must be the reassurance she needs. Suddenly, we're kissing as if we have to make up for lost time.

As if this moment is going to vanish into thin air and we want to make the most of it.

I grip her thighs, my hands moving higher until I reach her shorts. I flick the button to undo them.

"Should we go upstairs?" she asks. "What if your grandma comes back?"

I let out a boisterous laugh and nod.

"It's probably a smart idea."

She hops off me, grabbing my hand and pulling me up. She runs up the stairs, and holy shit, I've never felt so euphoric.

We dash into my room, and I close the door.

With our hands still locked together, I pull her back, turning until her back hits the door.

There are so many things I could say to her right now, but all of it can wait. *Kissing* her, *tasting* her, *feeling* her can't.

I squat, gripping the back of her thighs, and jerk her up to wrap her legs around me as I press my lips to her neck. Suspended between me and the door, she wraps her arms around my neck to hold on.

"Your skin is so soft," I say between kisses.

"I love your lips on me," she breathes. She uses her hands to make me look at her. "I can't remember the last time I felt this alive."

I seal our mouths together and take the opportunity to move us to the bed.

I lay her down slowly, continuing to kiss her as she scoots up on the bed. When she gets high enough, I settle my body between her legs.

My hand travels up her smooth legs, stalling at the hem of her shorts.

"I don't want to do anything you're not ready for," I tell her.

Her breathing is fast, but she smiles and says, "You're not."

Her shorts are still unbuttoned from downstairs, so I grab the zipper and slowly pull it down.

"Is this okay?"

"Yes."

She lifts her hips so I can remove her pants, leaving her in a simple black thong.

"Dove," I growl and slide down her body, kissing the inside of her thigh. I press my lips to one side and then the other before I place my hands where I'd just kissed her and press her legs open. "I like kissing you, but I think tasting you is about to become my new addiction."

I hear her inhaling as her back bows off the bed.

With one finger, I hook her panties to the side. The prettiest, lightest shade of pink shines back at me.

Oh yeah. I'm about to become an addict.

I know I should have more self-control, but the moment her fingers glide into my hair, I can't hold back.

"Ssshhhit," she hisses as my tongue licks her. I grab her legs and pull her close so she can feel my tongue and lips on her. Eating her. Memorizing her. Devouring her.

"Fuck, you taste amazing," I say and get back to it. "One taste and this pussy belongs to me—do you hear me?"

"Yes."

"This is mine now. I don't share."

"It's yours," she pants the moment my tongue touches her

again. I use two fingers to spread her open so that I can taste every single inch of her.

"Tobias," she says and pulls my hair. "Tobias."

Just as she sucks in a breath, her orgasm rocking through her, I slide a finger inside her and hook it, my tongue joining it, prolonging every last ounce of ecstasy for her.

When her body slowly stops shaking, I climb up her and press myself against her.

With the taste of her still on my lips, I kiss her.

I kiss her hard.

Her hand moves to my jeans. She flicks my belt open like a pro and then slides her hands inside.

"Oh my god," she says the moment her hand grabs ahold of me.

"Oh my god," I repeat and suck in breath.

She moves her hand slowly, and I swear I grow bigger the longer she touches me. Her other hand works back and forth to take my pants off.

When they get to the middle of my butt, I pull back and strip them the rest of the way off, yanking my shirt off with them.

"Lay on your back," she says.

I grin, thinking of that very first scene she wrote, and do as I'm told.

But then she begins to crawl down my body. I stop her.

"As much as I would love for you to put my cock in your mouth, it's not happening tonight."

"It's not? But you just made me … forget where I was."

I grin. "Good."

"So, if you don't want that, what do you want?"

I cup her cheek and pull her to me for a kiss.

"I want you to sit on my dick and ride me until we both see stars. And when we're done with that, I'm going to bend you over the side of the bed, slide back inside of you, and make you forget your name."

She fights a smile by biting her lip.

I reach for it with my thumb. On second thought, maybe I do want to see this lip wrapped around me.

The thought doesn't get too carried away before she's doing exactly what I told her to do.

She removes her underwear, whips off her shirt and crawls on top of me. Her bare center rubs against mine as she unclips her bra.

Instantly, my hands massage her breasts.

"Everything about you is amazing."

"You're just saying that because we're naked in bed."

"No, I'm not. I've never seen anything so perfect."

I lift my hips, encouraging her to move. She takes the hint, her hips moving back and forth, back and forth.

When I'm not sure how much longer I'll last, I reach for my jeans, retrieving a condom from my wallet.

Nat watches me with hungry eyes. I begin to sheath myself, but she takes over for me, pushing it down to my balls and then rising to her knees.

She holds me to her opening and slowly, oh so painfully slowly, lowers herself down on me.

I have to take small breaths.

"You're so fucking tight. Oh my god. I'm not … hold on, don't move," I say and hold her hips until she's all the way seated.

"You feel so good." She moans, her hand on my chest as

her nails dig into my skin. "How is this possible? I've never felt the way I do right now."

Before she can say anything more, I pull her down for a kiss. As soon as I start to move my hips, she matches my rhythm.

She sits up tall, grabbing the headboard to hold on while I crunch up, my gaze falling on the way I slide in and out, in and out.

Shit. This is like nothing I've ever experienced.

This is heaven.

Pure fucking bliss.

I circle my thumb against her clit, and the simple touch sets her off. She cries out, her hips moving faster and faster until my body has no choice but to follow behind her, my orgasm tearing through my body at the feel of her clenching over me.

This. I could get used to this.

And who better to do it with than my best friend?

CHAPTER TWENTY-SIX
NATALIE

I'm not a cuddler.

Or at least I didn't think I was.

I notice two things the moment I wake up. The first is the warm body that has me trapped under his arm and pulled tight against his chest. The second is the way my body aches, remembering everything that happened between us last night.

I slept with my best friend.

Not just slept.

I had sex with him.

With Tobias Banks.

And in a moment where my mind should be racing with worry over how this could go wrong, it's not.

Instead, I'm trying not to breathe too hard, thinking of all the ways I want last night to happen again and again and again.

I turn gently under his hold until we're face-to-face.

Am I worried about morning breath?

A little.

Am I mesmerized by the sweet yet sexy face in front of me?

Oh yes.

I reach up to cup his cheeks, letting my thumb brush over his stubble. He always has a little scruff, but I bet he'd look great with a full-faced beard.

My gaze takes in his chiseled jawline, the scar, now faded, on his chin that he got our first year out of college from an innocent volleyball game, the way his eyebrows look more groomed than mine, the way his plump lips are calling to me.

They've never called to me the way they are now.

I know how soft they are, but I want to touch them again.

I lean in, wondering if he'd like me to wake him with kisses. I know my best friend Tobias, but more-than-friends Tobias—now that's a completely different person to me.

"You better be planning to kiss me right now."

I hold back my smile, biting my lip as his eyes flash open.

"I was thinking about it."

"Don't think too hard, Dove. If it's something you want, it's something I want."

Oh, is this cheesy line Tobias?

"Hmm, is that so?"

"Very," he says just before his hand slides from my hip to my backside and jerks me against him. "Now, tell me what you want this morning. A kiss, a hug, my face between your legs eating you and licking you until you can't think anymore?"

I swallow and nod. "That one."

I assume he's going to pull an *are you sure?* or *you got it!* line, but instead, he lifts the sheets and crawls under.

He grabs my thighs and spreads them, causing me to shift to my back all in one move.

My body temperature instantly spikes, so I flip the sheets down to look at him.

With his head between my legs, he grins up at me.

"Sleeping without clothes is officially a requirement for you."

Then he places one long, slow lick against my core. My back starts to bow, but he reaches up to place his forearm over my hips, holding me down.

Then he eats as if he's a starved man and I'm the only thing that can refuel him.

"Fuck," I say quietly, running one hand through my hair while the other pulls at the hair on Tobias's head.

"Say more," he instructs. "Tell me how you want it."

I take a moment to focus on my breathing. How do I want it? Is he kidding me?

"I want it just like that."

"Like this?" he asks, pulling back to slide two fingers inside me.

"Oh yes."

"And this?"

He leans back in to suck my clit as his fingers twist and turn, enticing my orgasm out of me.

"Tobias," I breathe. "I'm close."

He picks up pace, his fingers scissoring inside of me to make room for his tongue.

"Fuck. Fuck." I close my eyes, little stars taking over the backs of my eyelids. I grab a pillow and place it over my mouth to let out the small scream I've been holding back.

As soon as my body calms down and I toss the pillow back to where it laid, I find a grinning Tobias watching me.

"How in the fuck did I let a sight like that get by me for the last ten years?"

I'm lying in the middle of the bed under his gaze, completely naked, and all I can think about is how I can make him feel the high coursing through my veins right now.

"Lie down," I say, and his eyes widen.

"You don't have to do anything for me. That was more for me than it was for you, I promise."

I let his words float between us for maybe thirty seconds before I sit up on my knees.

"I said, Lie. Down."

This time, he does as he's told and lies on his back. I crawl over him and then lower his boxers down his legs.

"If I'm sleeping naked, you're sleeping naked. Got it?"

He nods.

"Stop smirking."

"I can't," he says with a laugh. "I'm so fucking happy right now. Smiling is the result of that."

To this I laugh, but the giddiness of the moment is gone as soon as I sit on his lap, rubbing myself over him, letting him feel how wet he's made me.

"Shit, Nat, that's nice. That's really fucking nice."

I lean forward, keeping my slow and steady rhythm over him.

"I didn't realize you liked the word *fuck* so much," I whisper in his ear and then bite it gently, tugging it as I move my hips faster.

"I can't help it." He groans. He holds my hips as he lifts

his, increasing the friction between us. "You make me feel feral."

"We've spent one night together."

"That's all it took."

His hips jerk, pressing his hardness against me and causing me to flip over. He lands smoothly between my legs, holding one of them against his biceps.

"This is how I want you," he says. "Think of how deep I could get like this."

His eyes latch onto mine as if he needs approval.

I nod.

"Good," he says, grinding his hips into me one more time before he grabs a condom.

I hear the jingle of his belt and then a quiet "Fuck."

Leaning up on my elbows, I ask, "Is everything okay?"

His head drops. "I only had the three condoms we used last night. I swear I thought I had more."

"Oh, just three," I tease, and he shakes his head.

I'd suggest that we go without, but we just erased one line over the past few days. It might be smart to wait before we erase another.

"Well, it's a good thing we're going home today, isn't it?"

"Home?" he repeats and nods. "Yeah, pack your bags. Now."

He moves quickly, grabbing his clothes and tossing them into his suitcase.

"Slow down, Casanova."

He pins me with a look. "You know, a punishment might be in the cards for you if you keep that up."

I move, naked I might add, for the adjoining bathroom. "Can that be done in the shower?"

"Don't tease me." His head drops back.

"What? You're not up for the challenge?"

He drops his bag and stalks toward me with a dark look in his eye.

"Bathroom. Now."

I grin and do as I'm told.

I like to be my own boss, but when it comes to sex with Tobias, that's a different story.

* * *

As soon as we're back in Wind Valley, Nora calls to tell me that one of our authors accidentally hit publish on her new release a week early. We need to get packets out stat, so I rush to her house. We could have done it over the phone or by email, but working together is so much more efficient.

A couple of hours and lots of apologies later, the release blast is underway.

Nora sits back and blows out a long breath. "How was Lovers?"

"It was good."

"Just good?"

"Yep."

About a minute goes by before she taps the back of my chair.

"What's up?" I ask, spinning to face her.

She's got the baby in her arms and is swiveling her chair left to right slowly to keep her asleep.

"What did you do in Lovers?"

There is suspicion in the way her brown eyes stare me

down, but I don't give in. There is absolutely no way she could know anything that happened between Tobias and me.

"We ate good food, went to the fall festival each night, had cake for Grandma Betty's birthday, danced, and just hung out. Actually, it was exactly what I needed."

Especially the sex.

God. I cannot remember the last time I had sex like that.

Sex that not only engaged my entire body but my mind too. Instead of thinking of ways to make each of us reach the finish line, my mind was looking for ways we could do it over and over. To make it last.

I've never had sex like that.

"That's it?"

I think for a moment.

"Oh," I say and hold up a finger. "I caved and decided to read Tobias's first bestseller."

Which I did and didn't tell anyone. Not even Tobias.

For the record, he talks just as dirty in bed as he does in his books.

"Did you now?" Nora grins. "Did you like it?"

"I loved it," I say and then laugh. "It reminded me why I stopped reading them back in college."

"Did you stop reading this one?"

"Nope."

"What changed?"

I spin my chair back to face her.

"What's going on?" I point at her. "Why are you asking me so many questions?"

"Nothing." She shrugs and looks away.

"Nora."

"Nothing," she says, but this time she laughs. "I just want

you to be happy, and I've just been worried about you is all. I love that you and Tobias are back to being friends again. He's good for you."

"I think so, too."

I know I told Tobias we shouldn't tell anyone about us, but I'm going to combust if I don't tell at least one person.

I open my mouth, but she beats me to it. "It's probably a good thing that you two never dated or anything."

Okay, that was not what I was expecting.

"Why do you say that?"

"Because. What would happen if you two became an item and then stopped? Would it be weird? Would you still be friends? Would you be heartbroken? Would he? What if—"

"We had sex," I blurt out before she can go on. "All those questions you just asked be damned. We did it."

Nora's eyes grow to a size I've never seen before, and her bottom lip drops open.

"Say something."

She just keeps looking at me as if I were Ursula and she can no longer speak.

"What does this mean?" she says quickly, her voice low.

I shrug. "I'm not sure yet."

"How can you not know?"

"Because … it's complicated."

"I'll say, but oh my god!" she yells. "I have been waiting for this moment for years."

"Okay, it wasn't that dramatic, and what about all those things you just said?"

"Oh, pshh that. I was just trying to be a good friend and not let you stress over it the way I know you would, but oh my god! Was it a one-time thing? Do you think you'll keep doing it? Are you still going to find an apartment? I have so many questions."

"And I have zero answers."

"How?" Her hand slaps the top of the desk, and her baby startles. "I'd be wanting to know everything as soon as possible."

I shrug. "I don't know. I just … this is Tobias. I get this feeling that I don't need to be worried about anything."

Nora grins. "Yeah, you're probably right. You two may have been blind all this time, but your friends weren't."

"Yeah, that brings up another great point. We aren't going to tell a lot of people. Actually, you might be the only one who knows."

Her eyes widen again.

"Well, that's one way to keep things from getting boring."

She twists back to her computer.

To keep things from getting boring?

Is that what happened with Griffin?

Did he get bored with me and cheat?

Oh my god.

CHAPTER TWENTY-SEVEN
TOBIAS

"What's our plan to send you to Colorado next month to open the new location?"

I pause my writing and look over the screen at Simon. It wasn't that I forgot we were opening the new location. It's that I've been happily distracted.

The last couple of days since Natalie and I have been back in Wind Valley have been ... shoot, I can't explain it. Saying they've been the best days of my life is too cliché, but that's exactly what they have been. Every touch, kiss, hug, look, you name it, is natural between us. Yes, it's physical now, but the rest—the morning routines, the dinners we've cooked together, and all the moments in between are effortless. Our friendship has always been this way, but now—hell, it's like we found a part of us that we didn't know was missing, and we finally know where we belong.

"I go when it's ready—that's the plan," I tell him. I might not be looking forward to being away from Natalie so soon, but we do both work jobs where we can be anywhere, so I don't see why she couldn't come with me since I'm there for only a couple of weeks.

"Okay. You just seem like your head is in another place these days, so I wanted to check in."

"No, yeah, sorry about that. I'm focused, even if it might not seem that way."

Which is true. I've handled emails, messages, and various phone calls here and there. This area of my life is simple, so it doesn't take a lot out of me. Especially since once the contracts were signed, the renovations started quickly, and things are going smoothly. After all, the building was ready, and it was mostly cosmetic changes.

"Good."

"Perfect."

"I'm glad we went for the one with the apartment. Even though we haven't really dabbled in residential real estate yet, this is a great place to start."

"I agree," I say, my focus balancing between him and the novel in front of me.

With the idea of taking a trip to Colorado with Natalie on my mind, I reach for my phone to text her.

TOBIAS

I have to go to Colorado next month for work. I'll probably be there for a couple of weeks. Do you want to come with me?

DOVE

I won't be a distraction?

Oh, you will, but I can't imagine anything
better.

DOVE

Does this mean we need to tell our friends?
Won't they be suspicious?

I hop up from my seat, ready to take this conversation to the
back room where I can call her, but Natalie walks through the
front door before I even have time to excuse myself.

"What are you doing here?" I ask. I start to greet her with
a kiss, but her focus settles on Simon.

"I thought I could work with you guys here for a bit. Keep
things exciting on the work front."

"Of course." I move my things to make room for her.

I don't miss the way Simon is watching me carefully.

"Can I talk to you for a moment in the back?" I ask Natalie.

"Oh, sure, yeah."

She follows me to the back room, where I close the door
behind us and then push her against it to kiss her deeply.

"How can a couple of hours without kissing you feel like
an eternity?" I ask.

She laughs, rolling her eyes as she pushes me back. "Did
you bring me back here to make out?"

"No," I answer and then raise one eyebrow at her. "Is that
why you came with me? I can change my answer."

All she does is shake her head.

I take a seat on the edge of the desk. "No, I came back
here to finish the conversation we were having over text."

"Oh, about telling people?"

"That's the one," I say and bop her nose. I follow that up by grabbing her hips and pulling her to me. She rests her arms around my neck, and I wrap mine around her hips. "I think we should tell them when you're ready to tell them."

"So that means you want to tell people?"

"It means I'm ready for people to know you're mine and mine only, yes."

"Hmmm, a little possessive, are we?"

"Slightly."

Her head falls back on a laugh. I press my lips to her bare neck, kissing from her collarbone to her ear and then pressing my lips to hers.

"Do you want to know just how possessive I can get?"

Her eyes meet mine as she takes in a breath.

"Here?" she asks on a whisper.

My hand moves to the button on her shorts in response.

"You can tell me to stop," I tell her.

"As if I'd ever want that."

I flick her shorts open and jerk them down, turning her around.

I pull her back against me, sliding my hand around to her slink into the front of her panties.

She's standing while I sit on the desk, but as soon as I slide a finger inside of her, her legs buckle, and she rests her weight on me.

"Do you like that?" I whisper in her ear.

She nods. "Yes, but I don't want to play today. I just want you inside of me."

I'd never refuse to give her what she wants, so with one

hand still playing between her legs, I use the other to undo my pants. I lift off the desk enough to slide them off. I grab a condom from my wallet before they drop to the floor.

After I've rolled on the rubber, I stand, rotating her to face me. I pick her up, her legs wrapping around me. Then I back us up to the wall, and as soon as I find my footing, I adjust our bodies so I can slide inside her.

"Ohhhh," she says as she takes all of me. "This angle is nice."

"Nice?" I repeat. "What did I tell you about calling me nice?"

"Hmm, I don't know," she teases and bites her lip. "You might have to remind me."

"Oh, I can't do that." I pull out only to slam back in.

I spend the next ten minutes making sure she never forgets what calling me nice will get her, and honestly, by the time we're putting our clothes back on, I'm starting to think that she should call me nice more often.

"So, I was thinking of the new location and something we should add," Simon says once Natalie and I are both seated back out in the open area.

"What's that?" I ask.

"Soundproof walls."

Huh.

I guess Simon knows.

I sneak a look at Natalie. She and I both erupt into laughter.

"God," he groans. "The honeymoon phase is the worst."

"Only when it's not you," I say and pull Natalie close to kiss her forehead.

Simon calls this the honeymoon phase, but I have a feeling this is exactly how Natalie and I will always be together.

Carefree, happy, and falling quickly in love.

CHAPTER TWENTY-EIGHT
NATALIE

"I'm pretty sure if you can't find a way to keep your hands to yourself, everyone is going to know we're more than friends before we get a chance to tell them."

Tobias kisses my neck one more time before he unlocks his arms from around me and steps back. He'd been hugging me from behind while I cut up more limes for the margaritas we're planning to serve.

"I didn't mean you had to stop; I was just stating the obvious."

He spins me around and pins me against the counter.

"Maybe we don't tell them. Maybe we just keep being us and that's how they find out. They just see it."

He presses his lips to mine, his hand at my right hip gripping tight. The moment I feel his other hand touch my left hip; I push him back.

He was about to lift me onto the counter, and as much as I'd love to let him take me right here, right now, sex four times before noon is more than enough. Not to mention our friends will be here soon.

"You're going to have to save that for later, Casanova."

He chuckles, backing away and opening the fridge. He pulls out the premade mix from earlier and sets it on the counter next to me.

"We should cancel."

I let out a laugh.

"We are not canceling. As much as I would love to let you strip me down to nothing right now, everyone loves your annual BBQ as much as you do."

He huffs.

"I'm serious, Tobias. Although I personally enjoyed them when they were earlier in the year. Like June or July. Why is this year so late?"

He shrugs.

"I guess because even though I never admitted it, I hated seeing you and Griffin together. I would never not invite you, so the longer I waited, the longer I didn't have to see you with him."

It's still mind-blowing how different our lives were just a month ago. I hate that he felt that way.

"Well, that's not something to worry about anymore."

"No?" he asks teasingly.

"No. All we have to worry about now is getting bored."

I sneak a glance his way, but he doesn't have a chance to reply before his front door opens and Zane and Willa walk in.

"Finally," Zane says right from the start.

Willa sets a couple of bags of goodies down and gives me a hug.

"He's been waiting for this night for months."

Tobias slugs Zane's arm.

"Miss me?"

"No, but I'm ready for some games and to name someone's book this year."

Last year, I was the reason Tobias lost. He's yet to have a book release since then, but when he does have one ready, the guys get to name it.

They started this tradition around the same time I met Tobias.

The BBQ has a set number of games, and whoever loses the most has to let the other guys name their next book.

Oh no, what if Tobias's next book is the book we wrote together?

Figures. That's karma for being the reason he lost last year.

Quickly, the rest of the group shows up and we get on with the night. It starts to rain, so we have to move the last couple of games inside the house. There are disagreements, a treasure hunt that lasts way too long, and more stolen kisses than I can count.

When all is said and done and Tobias and I have redeemed our reputation from last summer, everyone gathers in the living room and kitchen area for one last drink and dessert.

"Now, before everyone leaves, we have an announcement," Tobias says and looks at me.

Gosh, this seems so silly to have to tell them this way, but they've all been rooting for us, so it seems fitting that we make it a full-blown announcement.

"Did you finish your book?" Hero asks.

"Did you already get a publishing deal? Or are you publishing independently?" Zane asks next.

"Are we supposed to guess, or are you just going to tell us?" Simon adds.

Tobias is about to share the news, but I do him one better. I push to my toes, grab his face, and kiss him.

Right there in front of all our closest friends, I kiss the man whom I should have been kissing back when we were dreaming of nights like these.

"Yes!" Beck shouts, and when I break the kiss, Tobias wraps his arms around my waist and pulls me in close.

From the corner of my eye, I spy Beck doing the same to Calla, kissing her head before he says, "All is right in the world, and our group is complete."

I try not to laugh at Beck's dramatics, but honestly, I love it. I can see why Calla fell for him even when she couldn't stand him, then married him. His heart is always in the right place.

"We should celebrate with dinner and drinks next weekend," Hero adds.

"We're having dinner and drinks right now," Graham says.

"Without kids is what he means," Nora adds.

Quickly, a plan falls into place for next weekend.

My face hurts from smiling so much in the last half hour, but I wouldn't have it any other way.

"Where are we having these drinks?" I ask once we've picked a night and time.

"At the Black Alcove bar," Zane says.

The smile that was hurting moments ago begins to falter.

The Black Alcove Bar is the best bar in Wind Valley. The food is good, drinks are great, the music sets a laidback vibe, and the people who work there are what keep you coming back.

The only problem is, I haven't been back for one specific reason.

Griffin's sister started working there a couple of weeks before the engagement party.

CHAPTER TWENTY-NINE
TOBIAS

I've never been happier writing a book than I am right now. That night at my grandma's house must have been a fluke because, as soon as Natalie and I gave our all, I swear, I've never felt more inspired. Maybe I was stressed over our relationship, and it blocked something inside me. Whatever it was, it's gone.

I feel lighter. Freer.

I watch Natalie's concentration as she types away on her laptop. For the last week, we have spent a couple of hours each night working on this story, followed by sleepless nights in each other's arms.

It's crazy to think that all the sappy and swoony and sexy words I've written over the years are now happening in my real life.

It's even crazier to think that I could have missed all of this.

Look at her. Her hair is in a mess on the top of her head, stray pieces framing her face. She curled it this morning, but one breakfast sex in the kitchen later and now her hair is a mess. Her eyes are practically glowing as she stares at her screen, and her lips—wow, don't even get me started on the way my imagination runs wild over those.

I'm one lucky, *lucky* man.

"If you keep looking at me like that, zero work will get done tonight, and after the last two nights, I want—no, I *need* to get these words in."

I chuckle. "Spoken like a true romance writer."

She fake bows at her seat. "Thank you."

She gets back to writing, but then groans. "Tobias, what is it?"

I rub my chin, grinning.

Gosh, I'm such a fool for her, it's not even funny.

"Have I told you thank you?"

"For what?" She sits back, crossing her arms.

"For reminding me why I love to write and showing me how easy it was to get that passion back."

"Ugh, don't be cute right now. I'm working."

"Why? Is it distracting?"

"Extremely."

I stand slowly.

"Don't," she laughs. "Sit back down right now."

"I'm not doing anything."

She shakes her head and crosses her arms. "You forget that I know you. You're up to something and by the look in your eyes, whatever it is, is going to keep me from finishing this chapter."

"What are you writing?" I ask, moving toward her.

"I love how you ask me this, knowing we plotted the book together."

"True, but it's normal for me to be writing the planned scene when a new one takes over, giving the chapter a better flow than the original one."

I sit on her desk and reach for her face.

She smacks my hand away.

"Maybe you struggled to write before because you were too distracted by the world around you."

Nah, I think it was because I didn't have Natalie in my life the way she deserved to be.

"Trust me. I'm more distracted now, and I'm getting more down."

She scoots her chair away from me, smirking.

"Five hundred more words."

I glance at her screen and suddenly crack up.

"I don't remember agreeing to a sex scene here."

"Well," she tosses her hands up, letting them slap her thighs when they drop. "Sex isn't always planned okay? And people get turned on at random moments of their day. Hence, he just told her he has to go back to the East Coast and the thought of him leaving made her go crazy."

"I like that angle. Feel free to finish the scene."

"Are you going to move?" she asks coyly.

I shake my head. "No."

"You're just going to watch me write?"

I volley my head. "I was thinking we could test your focus."

I grab her chair by the arm and yank it toward me. She gasps, but quickly pulls it together when she's right in front of me and I lean down until our lips are just a brush away from each other. "Write out what you want him to do to her, and I'll do it to you at the same time."

She guffaws. "Yeah, okay."

I raise a brow in challenge.

"You're serious?" she asks.

"When it comes to touching you in any form, I'm dead serious."

I press my lips to hers, trapping her lip between my teeth gently before I pull away.

The smallest whimper comes from her.

"Finish the scene, Natalie," I tell her and get to my knees in front of her.

She closes her eyes as I run my hands up her legs, inching her flowing skirt higher and higher. I hear her inhale when one hand dips in between her thighs and swipes against her underwear.

"Tell me what to do."

"I want you to …"

"Write it as you tell me."

She groans, moving the chair to face her computer. I move with her and when I hear the click of the keyboard, I sneak one finger under her thong and press it against her clit.

"Fuck," she breathes, but she keeps writing.

"Come on, Dove. I need you to tell me what to do next."

"Lift my hips to remove my underwear."

I do as I'm told.

"Now scoot me down to the edge of my chair."

Again, I follow directions.

"Spread my legs."

Done.

"Now, eat."

I spread her thighs even wider and do as she commands. The moment my tongue presses the first long stroke to her core, she stops typing. I'd tell her to keep going, but my mouth is busy, and I don't particularly care about the book at this moment.

I flick my tongue faster, listening to her breathing increase. She lets out a moan, and I add a finger.

"Tobias," she moans, trying to lean back, but she can't.

I pull away quickly, grabbing her at the waist and taking her with me to the floor. I place her on her knees on each side of my face, never taking my hands off her.

She tries to move, but I stop her.

"I'm not done yet," I growl.

"But you won't be able to breathe."

"Don't you worry about me. Just find something to hold on to, and when you're ready, ride my face the way you want to."

"Tobias," she begins to scold me, but I get back to work, stopping all the words on her tongue.

"Shit," she says. "Why does it feel so much better this way?"

I continue to flick my tongue, bring my fingers into the mix until I feel her move above me. Her hips gyrate faster and faster, grinding on my face.

I almost laugh—she was worried I couldn't breathe.

I can breathe just fine, and honestly, if I couldn't, this would be exactly how I'd want to go out.

Her release hits her hard and fast, and as soon as she finishes, I sit up, placing her in my lap, with one leg on each side of me.

I swipe a hand over my mouth, loving the taste of her on my lips.

"Well, that is definitely not what my characters were doing in that scene."

"Good. This should have been better."

"Oh, it was much, *much* better."

She leans down to kiss me, and I know she can feel my erection through my jeans. Ready for more, she unzips my pants, releasing me from my boxers, slides on a condom, and slowly lowers herself onto me.

At this rate, this book will be just another in the pile of my unfinished novels.

She lifts herself slightly and drops back down on me.

"Fuck." She does this over and over until I'm coming inside of her and she's crying out my name.

Book? What book?

* * *

I'm the first one to The Space the next afternoon for our weekly writing session. That hasn't happened in weeks.

I get set up and start working on the next chapter of Natalie's and my book. We're almost done, and it blows my mind. A little over two months ago, we decided to write this book.

I didn't even write my first book in that time. Then again, I had no idea what I was doing or even where to begin.

With Natalie, I just got my outlines together, and we pieced the story together and decided to write every other chapter. She knows this business and what readers want, and I know how to structure the books. It worked for us and now—now I'm about to finish a book.

I'm about to finish a book.

I like repeating it because it's a moment I never thought I'd see again.

"I don't think I've ever seen you smile like that before," Simon says, joining me at the table.

I'm pretty sure I smile even bigger.

"Natalie and I are almost done with this book," I say with my head high, and I puff my chest.

"Seriously? That was fast."

"I know, but we found our groove, and it just took off."

"That's good. Do you think you'll write more books together?"

"Maybe." I like that idea. Perhaps I'll be a co-writer from here on out. "I like that idea."

He settles in with his computer.

"Outside of the book, how are things going with Natalie?"

"Things are good."

Really good, actually.

"That's good. Even if you and Natalie decide to write more books together, you should keep writing them alone too."

I nod. "I'm starting to think she's the only reason I'm finishing this book, so I don't know if I'll go back to writing alone."

"Yeah, but what if something happens between the two of you?"

"Like what?"

"I don't know. What if you break up?"

I let out a bark. "That won't happen."

"You're that sure?"

"It's Natalie, Simon. *My* Natalie. I know everything about her, and she knows everything about me. She's it for me."

His expression gives no hint to his thoughts, but the vibe he's giving off says he's not sure he agrees with me.

"What if something happens with you and Greer?" I ask, and he rolls his eyes.

"Fine. I get it. I just worry."

"Well, don't."

Like always, we quickly fall into a routine: work on the new location and then dive into writing for the day.

I open the document Natalie and I share, reading over her last chapter. I make a couple of notes for her and then chuckle quietly at her notes on how it's hard to write a non-sexy scene after I've not only kept her up at night in person but then she has to read my dirty talk, and all she wants to do is keep going with a spicy scene.

I leave my own note that perhaps our next book could be a novella about a sex addict. That way, she can write her heart out with sex.

I read the ending to her chapter again, but for some reason the fourth time I read it, it makes me pause.

I never imagined that the three of us would be a family. This moment has always been a dream of mine, and now that I have it, I'm scared it won't be enough. That I won't be enough. That he'll get tired of this small-town life and want more. I've never been happier, but if I'm not careful, he's going to get bored with me and leave us behind. How do I guarantee my own happily ever after?

Natalie made a comment about me getting bored with her just before everyone arrived for the BBQ last weekend too.

I lean back and rub my chin. Is this our heroine, or is this Natalie talking?

CHAPTER THIRTY

NATALIE

My heart has been uneasy since the moment the group mentioned going to the Black Alcove for drinks last weekend.

What if Griffin's sister is working?

What if she says something to me?

Would she say something to me?

Plenty of time has passed since Griffin and I called off the engagement, but still, no one prepares you for this part. When you don't just risk running into the ex but the ex's family as well. Even though I'm not the one at fault, I have no doubt that they hold a grudge against me.

"Are you okay?" Tobias asks as I hesitate in the bathroom. I've been running my hands through my hair for at least five minutes to loosen my curls. At this rate, they'll be flat before we even make it out of the house.

"I'm good."

"As you would say, you forget that I know you." He wraps his arms around my torso, kissing the side of my head and smiling at our reflection in the mirror.

"Do I ever tell you how beautiful you are? How amazing you are? How lucky I am?"

I press my lips together.

"You do, but I like hearing it."

"Then I'll do it more often. Now, what's on your mind?"

I shift on my feet, looking away for a brief moment. When I finally bring my gaze back to his, I say, "Griffin's sister works at The Black Alcove."

He nods once. "Oh, I didn't know that."

"You're not supposed to know that."

"Well, I wish I had known before we made plans there."

"We can't pick a new favorite bar based on where my ex's family works."

"No, but we could have for one night."

I blow out a breath. "No, no. I'll be okay. This was bound to happen. I have to get used to the fact that I could run into them."

He rubs the back of his neck. "Do you want me to keep some distance?"

"What? Why?"

"I don't know. Because he was obsessed with the idea of us being more than friends, and now that we are, maybe it'll trigger her."

I try not to beam a giant smile.

"You could never keep your hands off me, and I never want you to. I'm allowed to be happy. I don't want to keep us a secret from anyone. Ever."

He smirks and then kisses my forehead. His hands go to my hips, lifting me onto the countertop. He nudges my legs apart and stands between them.

"So, you'd let me do this?" he asks, one hand sliding

slowly up my inner thigh as he rests his forehead against mine.

Instantly, my breathing picks up, and I hold back a moan.

"I mean," I breathe, "maybe we can have some rules while we're in public."

"Damn," he says, stopping his hand.

I unbuckle his belt.

"But we aren't in public yet." I kiss him hard.

That's all the fuel he needs. He pulls me to him, so his erection is pressed exactly where I need and want him most.

I put on a fall flowy dress for tonight, so the only thing that separates us is a measly piece of thin and now-wet fabric.

"I love it when you go after what you want."

"Do you?" I ask, pulling him free from his jeans and gliding my hand up and down his length. He grows bigger under my touch, and this time, there is no holding back my moan. I drop my head back—oh, how much I want him. His lips are like magnets to my neck as he kisses and sucks, finally sliding a finger past my thong and inside of me.

"Fuck, baby. How is this possible? How is it like this anytime we're together?"

"Because it's you," I remind him. "I've never wanted someone the way I want you every single day."

He kisses me again, biting my bottom lip and holding my head in place with his free hand. He kisses like he can't get enough of me. Of my mouth, my tongue, as if he wants to memorize every inch of me with his own.

"We'll be late if we keep this up," he says.

"They're our biggest supporters," I reply. "They'll wait."

He chuckles but then hastily yanks my panties down my

legs, tossing them somewhere on the floor behind him before returning to position himself at my entrance.

"I want you bare. Is that what you want?"

"Yes." I pant as he flicks his tip against me, rubbing it over my center but never actually entering me.

He captures my lips with his once more, his tongue sliding past our lips and into my mouth at the same time he thrusts into me.

I moan into his mouth and then lock my heels behind his back once he's all the way in.

I don't let him pull back.

"Hold onto me," he says.

I grip his shoulders and grind my hips up and down, then side to side.

"Oh, fuck, Natalie. Yes. Like that."

I keep the pace for another minute, but my arms start to shake from holding myself up. Tobias can feel my grip loosening; he picks me up and walks me to the bed. Laying me down, without ever breaking contact, he stays standing. He pulls my legs up, resting my heels on his shoulders.

"Deep and slow is how you want it?"

I nod.

"Then that's what you'll get."

He circles his hips as if he's slowly trying to stretch me and make room for more.

My back bows at the feel of him inside of me, giving me what I want. He always does, and the idea of him always putting me first turns me on even more. I'm about to reach down to play with my clit because I need more, but his thumb beats me to it and another finger slides in over his cock.

I gasp.

"Do you like that?"

"Yes," I breathe.

"Do you want more?" he asks, but I don't answer him. The feeling is better than I could imagine. Him hitting me as deep as he can go, his finger curling and rubbing me to oblivion.

"Right now, you have my cock and one finger inside of you. Do you want more?"

I run my hands through my hair and pull, as if it's going to help me to keep from losing control.

I nod quickly. I want whatever he's willing to give me.

He pulls out quickly, flips me over, lifts my hips, and thrusts back inside me before I can muster up any words.

Sex with Tobias is always exciting, and switching positions makes me last longer than I expect. It's like he knows when I'm about to explode, so he switches things up to draw it out.

I'd beg him to let me come if the sensation of his touch and the idea that he loves my body weren't so intoxicating.

He slides in and out of me, his hips moving faster and faster, our bodies slapping together. Slow sex is amazing, but rough sex, the sex where he loses control because he just can't get enough of me fast enough, is my favorite.

I balance on one hand, reaching back with my other as I look at him.

He grins.

"Yeah, baby, watch me take you. Watch your pussy make me come."

And just like that, his pace quickens, and he lets out the deepest, sexiest moan, his head tilting back and his throat on display. The pure ecstasy of his reaction sends my body following right behind him.

I cry out, his hand rubbing my clit again to draw it out for as long as possible.

Too soon, we both come down from our high.

I flip over to my back to catch my breath, and Tobias lies next to me. I turn my head to look at him with a smile, and he does the same.

I've never been happier than I am right now, with him.

* * *

I let out a small breath as soon as we step into the bar. The coast is clear.

For now, anyway. I don't see Griffin's sister anywhere, but I did see her car outside, so I know she's here. A part of me wishes I saw her first thing. To get this moment over with.

"Are you doing okay?" Tobias asks, his hand on my lower back as we make our way to the back table at the bar, where we spot Greer and Simon.

"I'm good. Maybe she'll just see you first and forget all about me. I'm probably overthinking all of this."

"You're not."

"I could be."

He leans into kiss my temple.

"Well, I'm here with you, so there isn't anything to worry about."

I squeeze his hand.

"We thought maybe you two were going to bail on us," Greer says as we take a seat at the table with them.

"Nope. Just running late."

"For two people who love to be on time, I find that odd."

Greer elbows Simon in the hip.

"Sorry." He looks at us and smiles. "I like this side of you two."

I roll my eyes, and Tobias just holds my hand tighter.

Then I spot her. The hair on my neck instantly stands up as she glares across the bar at me.

"Ignore her," Tobias whispers in my ear.

I nod and then focus on our friends.

Nora and Hero arrive, followed by Beck and Calla, and soon enough we're a couple of drinks in, with plates of appetizers on the table.

"I'm going to run to the restroom," I tell Tobias.

"Need a hand?" He smirks.

"Not from you."

I hate that I look over my shoulder more than once on my walk to the bathroom, but I don't see Cassie. I take care of business and push out the door to return to the table.

I was definitely overthin—

"I can't believe you," a voice snaps beside me. I don't even have to fully turn to know who it is. She must have been waiting for me to leave my friends so that she could corner me.

"Hi, Cassie."

"Don't. Don't even pretend like we're still friends. We are far from it."

I nod and then sigh. "I know you're mad."

"No, you don't get to play the nice one. The calm one. You messed up, Natalie. Big time."

What does that mean? He cheated on me. Not the other way around. Although, at this point, that might not be what he told his family.

"Look, Griffin and I are over, and I think it's—"

"And that guy, oooooh, ahhhh." She points over my shoulder, trying to find her words. I'm not sure why I keep standing here, because she's clearly mad, and this isn't going to go in my favor. Maybe it's because even though she is crazy, I did try to form some type of friendship with her. By her reaction, maybe she thought we were closer than I thought. Sure, I thought she'd be mad on her brother's behalf, but hurt, no. Yet her eyes are glistening.

"You two are stupid," she snaps.

"Is there a problem here?" Tobias walks up behind me, lacing his hand with mine. "I can hear you across the bar, and you're drawing attention."

Cassie glares at Tobias. "You two are unbelievable. I bet this was happening the entire time you were with my brother."

"It wasn't."

But now we know what he's been telling people.

"For your sake, I hope not. Because if it was, Tobias will be bored soon, too, and then just like my brother, he's going to find someone better who—"

"That's enough," Tobias says calmly in a clipped tone before I can. I don't need him to fight my battles, but I'm on the verge of tears, so it's nice to have someone in my corner right now.

"Go ahead. Defend her. Be who she needs you to be, because when you're tired and bored, you'll move on from her too."

"I said that's enough," Tobias says and turns me to walk away.

"I sure as hell hope you figure it out soon, Tobias. You know where to find me when you need some excitement in your life!"

"Don't listen to her," Tobias whispers in my ear. "I'm going to have a word with the manager when I see him next. She shouldn't be allowed to talk to customers this way."

"She's right, though," I tell him, grabbing my purse off the table. Nora eyes me but doesn't say anything. "What if you do get bored with me?"

"No. Don't listen to her, Nat. You've had my attention since the day I met you. If I were going to be bored, it would have happened by now."

My lower lip starts to shake. I know he's trying to lighten the situation with a little humor, but it's not helping. Yeah, friend Tobias never got bored with me, but what about boyfriend Tobias?

"Can we go home, please?"

He nods without another word, then pulls some cash from his wallet to leave with our friends. I hear him tell the others good night, but I don't know if they reply. Everything starts to blur under my tears.

I was starting to think I had things figured out, but now, I'm not so sure.

CHAPTER THIRTY-ONE
TOBIAS

Natalie hasn't spoken the entire car ride home. I know she's replaying Cassie's words over and over.

Bored?

Does she honestly think I'll get bored with her? That's impossible.

My life is nothing but amazing with her, and it's better than ever because she's in it.

I need to tell her that, but right now I'm afraid she'll think I'm just saying it to cheer her up.

Bored.

That one word pisses me off.

Not only because of what Cassie said, but because Natalie has implied this more than once, and I never once caught on to it enough to talk to her about it before now. She was basically telling me from the start that this was a concern of hers, and I never noticed.

I should have noticed.

Has she been worried this entire time?

Yeah, so it's only been a few weeks since we started fooling around, but we have known each other for years. She should know that she can trust me by now.

What does it say about us if she doesn't know that?

I pull into the garage and get out to open her door.

She beats me to it and then moves like a zombie into the house, setting her purse down and shrugging off her coat.

I rest my hand on her lower back.

"Do you want to talk about it?"

"No."

I take my coat off, too, hanging it up on the hook by the door. When I turn back around, she hasn't moved.

"She's wrong. Every word she said was wrong."

"No, it wasn't," she snaps and turns to face me. "He cheated on me. He was bored. I was boring to him."

I rest my hands on my hips. "He's an idiot, Natalie. There is nothing boring about you."

Her hands fly up, and she huffs. She marches past me and up the stairs, but I'm hot on her tail.

"Where are you going?" I ask, following her.

"I don't know."

"Dove, wait."

"And for the love of all there is in this world, will you just tell me why you call me Dove?"

I shake my head. If she weren't visibly upset, I might tell her. But this isn't the time for me to reveal that.

"Typical." She tosses her hands up again, heads into the bedroom, and opens the closet. She jerks the door so hard that it slams off the wall behind it.

"What are you doing?" I ask.

"Leaving," she says and grabs her suitcase.

"Leaving?" I grab her bag out of her hands.

"Stop. Give it back."

"You're not leaving. You're running."

"Because this is going to end eventually. It won't work out. It's better to call it now."

"It won't work out?" I repeat back to her. "How do you figure that?"

"Because we … the longer we let this go on, the harder it'll be when it ends."

She can't be serious right now.

"Why does it have to end?"

She sighs, reaching again for her suitcase, but I move so she can't grab it. She takes a breath and then looks me dead in the eyes.

"You don't want me, Tobias. You only think we should keep doing this because you're afraid to lose me."

"You're damn straight I'm scared to lose you."

I toss a hand into the air, turning away from her and then circle back.

"You," I gesture to her with my hand. "You're my best friend."

"I know," she says softly. "And you'll aways be mine, even if we aren't together romantically."

"No. This is not happening right now," I start to argue. She's scared, and I get it. But she's making a mistake, and I won't let her do it. I open my mouth to say more, but she beats me to it.

"We never talked about what being more to each other would mean. Or about where this will go. We didn't think things through. We just started being more and went with it."

She starts to pull clothes off the hangers. Did she ever

mean to make it more than what we were? Hell, it was more. It *is* more.

"We can talk about it now."

"I think it's too late for that," she says, refusing to look at me.

"Fine. Then you can listen. I don't see an end for us. For me, the end is each night you are with me, in my arms, in my bed. You are the last thing I see at night and the first thing I see when my eyes open every morning. Tonight, tomorrow, next month, next year, twenty years from now. You're it for me." I toss my hands up, waiting for her to say something. All she gives me is silence. "I'm sorry I didn't go about it the right way and that I didn't tell you fully how I felt the moment I felt it, but I'm telling you now. Don't go. Please."

The suitcase drops, and she starts to cry. I reach for her, feeling as if someone had just shoved a knife into my heart. She doesn't back up or try to step away; she just lets me hold her.

"Don't go," I repeat, kissing the top of her head as her tears soak my shirt.

"I'm scared you'll get bored of me." Her words are muffled into my shirt, but I hear them clearly.

Fuck.

Why didn't I talk to her about this sooner?

I pull back, crouching to eye level with her. I cup her face, kiss her, and then make sure she's focused only on me. "That will never happen."

"What if it does?"

"It won't."

"Do you promise?"

"Yes. Trust me, okay?"

She thinks about my words for a moment, then nods. We get ready for bed in silence, which I hate, but I let her take the lead on the night. When we climb into bed, she snuggles to me, so I assume the night has taken a toll on her, and she just needed a moment to let it all out. She falls asleep before me, but I stay awake for another hour.

Our first fight and we made it.

We made it.

Or so I thought.

By the time the sun rises in the morning, she's gone.

CHAPTER THIRTY-TWO
NATALIE

The night they met

I'm not the type of girl to follow a guy I just met into his bedroom. A room that's in a house he shares with a bunch of other guys to be more specific.

It's not a smart move, yet this boy—wow. I'm drawn to him.

"Is this the part where you tell me your last name too?" I ask, using the same teasing tone he's been directing at me all night.

He's a flirt.

I like guys who still take the time to flirt.

Of course, I'm not going to tell him that. I've already called him out for attempting to hit on me. What would he think if I suddenly changed my mind, and I want him to hit on me?

"Banks. Tobias Banks," he says with enough confidence to make me jealous.

The fall semester is supposed to start in just a matter of weeks, and I'm still trying to decide whether I should leave or not. Go home, call it a good effort, because college isn't for me. It didn't help me find what I was looking for or guide me in the direction I'm supposed to take with my life.

You know, all the things a young woman hopes to find.

But Tobias, oh, everything about him screams confidence. It's not coming off as cocky. It's more like "Hey there, follow me. I make goals and take action to get what I want" type of confidence. A man who put in the work and is proud to show it off.

Like right now.

I kid you not, if this boy pulls out a romance novel he wrote, I will very well melt right here on the floor.

A guy who writes romance and wants to shout it from the rooftop, or in our case, bring a random girl to his room to show it off, is definitely one to swoon over.

The moment we walk into his room, I hear Elvis's "Suspicious Minds" playing from somewhere. I make a quick scan of his tidy room—no radio, but there is a computer half propped open, so I assume that's where the music is coming from.

I love Elvis, like most people, but I don't mention it.

I'm here to see a romance novel, and I'm not about to let him get distracted.

"Your room is clean," I say instead. Why? I have no clue. Maybe because the guys I've hung out with never have a room this clean. I mean, what is that, lemon and spruce? Is that even a combination? And why do I feel like this room was cleaned by a professional?

Jesus, Natalie, why are you obsessing over the room?

I cross and uncross my arms. Then I pretend I have an itch on my upper arm as he watches me.

"Are you nervous?" he asks, sitting back on his desk, adding space between us.

I'm not sure why I notice it, but his giving me space calms me.

"A little," I admit.

He grabs the doorknob and opens the door completely. There's a couple making out in the hallway; beyond them are people waiting in line for the bathroom. One girl looks up at me and smiles.

"No problem. Let me just grab my book and then we can get back to the crowd. It's the only copy I have right now. Outside of my family, the boys, and now you, not many people know I write romance."

"Oh, and here I thought you were telling all the girls to impress them."

"Nope. You're the first. I must have been waiting for the right girl to talk to me. Should we head back out there?" he asks, holding the book in his hand.

I look between him and the girl who is now taking her turn for the bathroom.

"It's okay," I tell him and then close the door a little. "It's quieter in here, and you seem like a nice guy."

"A nice guy," he repeats, rubbing his chin as he crosses one ankle over the other. "Thanks, I guess."

"You don't like being called a nice guy?"

"I mean, if you consider the whole nice guys finish last thing, no, it's not exactly a trait I'd like connected to my name."

"Oh really," I say as we find our way back to the flirty

vibe we established before coming to his room. I sit on his bed and crisscross my legs. "Tell me what kind of traits you'd like connected to your name."

He chuckles and hands me a book.

Sure enough, it has his name on it.

"Wow, you really wrote this?" I flip the pages and then look at the back cover. "One moment changed their entire lives." I read the tag line at the top and then smile at him. "Okay, *okay*, I'm impressed."

I don't wait for his reply as I open to a random page and start reading quietly. I make it about three sentences before I snap the book closed.

"Tobias Banks! You write naughty books." I laugh.

My gaze scans him from head to toe. He's still standing away from the bed, but his attention is on me. I want to remember the smile on his lips forever.

A new song starts up, this one by the Black Pumas—he seems to have the same taste in music as I do—and I chuckle. "Okay, let me pick out new traits for you."

"After fifteen minutes of knowing each other?"

I nod. "Yes."

"Okay, let's hear it, but only if I get to pick yours too."

"Oh, now who's getting cocky?"

He shrugs. "What can I say? I have a way with knowing people's characteristics."

I roll my eyes, but I love that his comebacks are so quick.

"Hmm, Tobias Banks is driven and likes to have goals." I hold up the book. "Creative and realistic." I lean in close and whisper, "Everyone wants sex in their books, but they don't admit it. I mean, sex happens to everyone; it's the most realistic part of any story."

He chuckles.

"He's smart, and he trusts easily. He's also very organized, and he's very good with words."

"Not bad," he says.

"I'm not finished. He's also a nice guy." Tobias cringes. "With a dirty mind that may as well make him the modern-day Casanova."

He fake gags.

"Do not start that. The guys would never let me live it down."

"No problem. I'll be our secret."

"Thank you."

"Okay, do me."

His eyes widen, and his bottom lip drops.

"Not like that. Jeez, Casanova. Calm down. I mean my traits. What do you think they are?"

He chuckles but rubs the back of his neck and starts to move around the room.

"You're stubborn," he starts, and I just smile. It's not the first time I've heard that one. "You like a good sparring match in conversation, and you'll defend the people you love, no questions asked. You speak your mind and people probably mistake your honesty for crudeness far more often that they should. You don't make rash decisions. You need time to think the big things through but will take risks if they help point you in the right direction. Hence, you came up here with me to see my book. Oh, and you wish your room was as clean as mine."

I burst out laughing at his last line as if I weren't in shock. After just minutes of knowing me, he figured me out to a T.

"Am I right?"

I nod. "Scary right."

Finally, he sits next to me on the bed.

"I knew it. Are you going to Wind Valley University this fall?" he asks.

"Yes," I answer without thinking. What was it he said? I'm willing to take risks if it means pointing me in the right direction.

"Good. I hope I see you again."

I can feel my face heating before I look away.

"I'd like that."

And I would, because for the first time in months, I feel like I just made the right choice, and it didn't scare me. Leaving and never seeing Tobias again after tonight—now, that scares me.

Present Day

Leaving before Tobias woke up wasn't an easy choice to make, but I had to make one, and being around him … well, I can't think straight.

When did every choice in life become a debate?

Why is there this need to pick between right and wrong instead of just what you want?

I hate that somewhere in life, I lost myself. And just when I was starting to feel like I'd found myself again, something popped up to remind me to question if it is what I need.

My heart says *yes, go get what you want*, but the what-ifs stop me every single time.

What if it doesn't work?

What if I hurt him?

What if he hurts me?

What if he does get bored?

What if I love him and it ends and causes this domino effect on our friends, and they suddenly feel the need to pick sides?

What can't I just accept that I was happy?

I roll over on the bed in Nora's guest room. I've been here for a few hours now. I wasn't sure where else to go. I'm sure she's eager with questions, but I'm not sure if I'm ready to answer them.

I let out a groan and cover my eyes with my arm.

I'm out of a place to live twice in the last few months.

Well, not exactly. Tobias would never kick me out, and that makes my heart hurt even more. How can he be so sure of us? Why can't I feel that? What's holding me back?

"Knock, knock," Nora says, pushing the bedroom door open slowly. "Can I come in?"

"Of course."

I sit up on the bed and sit cross-legged. She's carrying a box in her hands.

"What's in the box?" I ask as soon as the door shuts behind her.

"I don't know yet. We're going to look through it together."

She drops the box to the bed and then sits, reaching in to pull out a polaroid camera.

I laugh and take it from her. "And to think these things are all the rage now."

"I know. Simon used to tease me so much during college for using one. Oh, look at this." Nora pulls out an old phone. The iPhones now are at least twice the size of the one in her hand.

"Can you imagine the pictures on that thing?"

Her eyes light up, and she starts to dig deeper into the box, looking for something.

"Yes!" she cheers, pulling out a charging cord and plugs it in. "We're going to find out."

While we wait for it to charge, one by one, we find random pictures or things from our college years. Me and her, old boyfriends, the boys with their first books, parties, and more.

"I don't mean to be this dramatic, but is there a reason you chose to come in here with this box?"

She shakes her head. "Just good timing, I think."

I roll my eyes as she hands me a picture of Tobias and the guys.

"What night was this?" I ask.

"I think it was Graham's first book release."

I look closer; it looks like Hero and Simon are barely holding him up.

"Oh yeah, the shots night."

Nora laughs. "College was fun."

"Even though you had to see Hero as much as you did."

"Yes. It's crazy to think that the night you met Tobias, I met Hero. Only Hero asked me out and then stood me up, and you put Tobias in a hard-core friend zone."

"I didn't put him in a hard-core friend zone," I defend myself. "He just never hit on me. Where else was I supposed to put him?"

"What if you had fallen in love back then?"

"Well, we probably would have broken up because we were kids, and he wouldn't be the best part of my life now," I tell her.

"Mm-hmm."

He really is the best part of my life. He'd love looking through this box with us.

Why is the idea of Tobias and me as more than friends so hard to accept?

I sigh loudly as the door to the room opens.

"Hey," Hero says, poking his head in. "I'm just going to order a pizza for lunch. Any requests?"

"Dessert pizza," I say with a big old smile.

"And for the main course?"

"Pepperoni."

"Crust?"

"Thick."

"Second pizza?"

"Hawaiian."

That's what Tobias would want. Even though he isn't here.

"Soda?"

"Water."

"Do you love Tobias?"

"Yes."

My head snaps up as Nora gasps. Hero slaps the doorframe as he leaves.

"What just happened?" I ask.

"You finally admitted that what you want is what just happened. Over a pizza order."

She keeps scrolling through her old phone as I think about the last thirty seconds. I do love him. I love him more than I've ever loved anyone. Maybe that's why I can't just accept it. Because if it did end, it would hurt the worst, and I'd never recover. But I know it would hurt worse if I never took a chance on him. On us.

You don't make rash decisions. You need time to think the big things through but will take risks if helps point you in the right direction.

I wasn't meant to go to his room that night to see a book. I was meant to go so that I could be with him.

Because I was meant to fall in love with him. The way I am now.

"Oh, I just found a video of you and Tobias," Nora says. The video starts to play in the background.

Why am I here? I should be with Tobias and working this out. We might not have all the answers figured out today, but I sure as hell won't get any closer to them if I'm not with him.

He's my person.

He's my best friend.

He's the man I fell in love with ten years ago.

I just didn't know it until now.

"Ahhhhhh, oooooo."

My gaze snaps to Nora's phone at the very clear sound of my own drunken voice. Oh god, what video did she find?

"Nat, stop swaying like that, I can't get the video to focus," Nora voice fills the screen as the blurry image evens out, revealing Tobias and me sitting next to each other on one of the end tables at his old college house. He's got his arm around me as I … I think I'm trying to sit-bop to the music, but I can't be sure at this moment. Tobias is looking down at me with a giant smile.

"Tobias, get her water," Nora's voice chimes in again.

"She's been drinking water for an hour now, Nora. I've got her."

"I'm sure you do," Nora says in a teasing tone. Tobias

turns to glare at her, but I grab his face and make him look at me.

"I have to tell you something," I say to him.

"What's that?"

"I ... I ..."

"Jesus, Nat." Nora hits me as we both stay glued to the phone screen. "Spit it out."

"Seriously, how drunk was I?"

"You ..." Tobias says in the video, his hand on my chin to gently force me to look at him. "Tell me. It's just me."

His voice gives me goosebumps.

"I dove you," I say and then turn to Nora, smiling into the camera. "Oh! Nachos," I shout and then run off.

"Natalie," Nora is yelling at me, but her camera is still on Tobias.

"Yeah, Nat," he sighs. "I dove you too."

"Holy shit," Nora whispers.

I grab my purse and run out of their house.

CHAPTER THIRTY-THREE
TOBIAS

Waking up alone after spending night after night waking up to the woman you thought you might spend forever with sucks.

I wanted to tell her I loved her. That I've loved her for as long as I can remember, even if I might not have known the depth of that love. The day she told me she "doved" me, I knew something changed between us. Honestly, I just thought I was the lucky college kid who'd found this amazing girl who wanted to be friends with me no matter what, but really, that had to have been the day I fell in love with her. Hell, I think I've been in love with her since the moment we met.

It sure as hell would have made the last ten years easier had I seen that.

I should have told her how I feel last night.

But I didn't.

I told her everything else except that.

Telling someone you love them in the middle of a fight seems wrong. Like a last-ditch desperate effort to convince someone to love you back.

I didn't want that.

She didn't deserve that.

But now that I'm lying here, staring at the side of the bed that should be filled with her smile and her laugh, I wonder if it would have made a difference.

I would have meant every word, but it was clear she was struggling to believe me.

Not once in our entire friendship did I give her a reason not to trust me.

Not once.

Everything changes when feelings get involved. When your heart is at risk of breaking.

I suck in a breath and roll to my back.

And let me tell you, it really does hurt.

I do get up to make some food—a broken heart still needs to eat. Well, mine does.

I make a BLT sandwich and grab the cheddar chips Natalie loves and sit by myself at the kitchen table. One of her sweaters is hanging off the chair across from me.

What's the right move here? Go after her, or give her space to figure this out on her own?

I want to find her and hold her and shake her, tell her to trust me, trust us, until she does. But I can't make that choice for her.

She'll come back for it, won't she?

Early afternoon is also a bust. I worked out. It was mediocre. My heart wasn't in it because Natalie took it with her wherever she went.

God, I'm pathetic.

She really doesn't feel the same?

I just can't wrap my head around it.

There's no way I could feel this way and not have it returned. Then again, being in love is tricky.

This is stupid.

I'm calling her.

This is not how we end. I'm not letting days or weeks go by. Hell, it's been six hours, and I'm not accepting this as over.

If she wants to see me committed to someone, she's got it. I'm committed to reminding her how special she is to me day in and day out. How baking frustrates me, but I'll do it every day of my life to make her those oatmeal cookies she likes. I'll get a cat, even though I can't stand them, just to make her happy. I'll wake up every morning to train for a marathon with her if she asks me to … again. I'm committed. From the smallest thing in our life to the biggest, I'm hers.

I grab my phone and pull up her name, calling her without a second thought.

Not talking things through is what got us into this. Got me into this. She wants me to be clear. I'll be as clear as fucking glass.

It goes to her voicemail.

"Fuck," I say.

I debate hanging up and calling her back over and over until she answers but decide to leave her message instead.

No more debating what I should and shouldn't do.

Love doesn't set the rules—we do.

"Natalie, it's me." I pause, letting the words sink in carefully before I say them. "I should have told you from the start that the feelings I have for you run so deeply that I never planned for us to end. That when we stood in my office, and I told you I was waiting for the one, I knew it was you, even if my heart and mind hadn't figured it out yet. My subconscious knew, though. That's why I've never dated long-term. There was a small piece in the back of my mind waiting for me to figure this out. And I did. Please tell me it's not too late." I take a breath, blowing it out slowly. "I didn't want to say this over the phone, but if this is the only chance I get, I'm takin—"

"Can I go first?"

My heart lurches at the sound of her voice, and I spin to find her standing behind me.

"Dove."

"Dove," she repeats with a sly smile. "Yeah, it gets the best of us, doesn't it? Makes us do crazy things." She steps forward. "Like run because we're scared of the unknown."

I end the call and take two steps to stand right in front of her.

Her hand cups my cheek.

"I'm sorry I left this morning, and I'm sorry about last night. I let my emotions get the best of me. You deserve better than that."

I let out a breath, closing my eyes and soaking in her touch.

"I should have talked to you sooner."

She nods. "Me too, but this whole new us is scary, and for some crazy reason, all my mind could think of was *how could*

Tobias Banks ever see me in any way other than his friend for more than a short time?"

"Oh, trust me, I can. I'll never see you in any way other than *mine*."

"So, can you forgive me?"

I nod and lace her hand with mine.

"I was about to confess my feelings to your voicemail and then search every part of this town until I found you and brought you home. Here. With me. Where you belong. Even when you're unsure of what happens next. Because I'm sure, and I'll remind you over and over until it sticks."

"It's sticking pretty good right now, but um, what's the one thing you wish you had told me the night we met?" she asks.

"Easy. That I was, in fact, hitting on you when I said come to my room to see my romance books."

She slaps my chest and lets out a playful laugh.

"I knew it."

"And also, that from that night, even after knowing you only an hour, I loved you. That I would love you for my entire life. I'm so sorry it took me this long to figure it out."

"You love me?" she asks, and her eyes start to glaze over. "Or do you *dove* me?"

I let out a loud laugh and then yank her body to mine, cupping her cheek the way she still holds mine. She figured it out.

"Both."

I crash my mouth to hers and kiss her like it's the first and last time all in one. She presses me back until I stumble and hit the couch. She lands on top of me and pushes herself up with her hands to look down at me.

"Promise me that if you ever start to get scared about us, you won't run," I tell her.

"I promise, but same for you, okay?"

She kisses me again, and I slip my tongue in her mouth and then pull her bottom lip between my teeth.

"If I've learned anything over the last ten years, it's this: you and me." I kiss her one more time because I want all her kisses, day and night. "You and me, Tobias and Natalie. We've always been right."

EPILOGUE
TOBIAS

Seven-ish Months Later

"Who was the first person you told outside of your family and close friends circle that you were a romance writer?"

Natalie reads out loud a question from the interview I did at the end of last summer.

She's leaning back in her chair, the sun shining down on her barely covered body as we soak up the sun on a beach in the Maldives.

The same trip I planned and gave to the girls for her bachelorette party. One way or the other, I was sending her on her dream trip.

Little did I know that it would be the trip where I propose to her.

But shhh, she doesn't know that fun fact quite yet.

"Are you listening?" she asks, turning to me.

I grin, waiting for her to go on.

"Yep. You've got my full attention."

As she should and always does.

"Do you remember your answer?"

"I do."

"Hmm, well, let's see what it is."

Her voice turns deep as she imitates me. "The first person I told I was a romance writer outside of my friends and family was a girl I'd met at a party." She stops talking, and when she goes on, her voice is normal again. "I'd known her for maybe thirty minutes but knew she was different. She was the kind of girl you meet and then work your ass off to keep in your life."

"Does this girl have a name?" she reads the next question. "Nat—" She pauses to take a breath. "Natalie Miller."

"And is this woman still in your life?" she keeps reading. "She is, and I'll make it my goal to see that she's there for the rest of my life."

She has tears in her eyes. "I was still with Griffin when you did this interview, wasn't I?"

"Yeah."

"But you knew. Even if you didn't *know* know, you knew."

"You're starting to sound like Beck."

She laughs. "He's starting to sound a lot smarter than I gave him credit for."

"Shhh, we might be thousands of miles away, but he will hear you."

"This is amazing, Tobias, and perfect timing since we just announced the release date of our book."

"Impeccable timing," I say.

"Truly," she teases me.

"Do you know what would make it even better?"

"Better?" she asks with a laugh. "You've got the cover

and center of L-Mag, your first book in years comes out in two months, and you're on a beach drinking fruity drinks with your best friend who doubles as your girlfriend." She turns to me with a giant smile. "What more could you want?"

"Well," I start, reaching into the only zipped compartment of our beach bag. I grab the small black box and slide off my lounger to my knee. "If that best-friend-turned-girlfriend wants to turn into my wife, that would be better."

Her eyes grow wider, and her hand covers her heart.

"Tobias," she whispers.

"I meant what I said. I will fight to keep you in my life until my dying day, but it would be a lot easier if you were my wife."

She bites her lip, and I let out a small groan.

"My life is not a life I want to live unless you are in it, Natalie Miller. Will you marry me?"

"Yes!" she shouts and then tackles me to the sand. I barely snap the ring box closed before I fall backward, and she smothers me with kisses.

The faint clapping of an audience behind us steals her attention.

"Oh, people are—OH MY GOD!"

I chuckle as she smacks my chest. "You invited everyone!"

I glance back at the group: Hero and Nora, Zane and Willa, Beck and Calla, Graham and Paige, and finally, Simon and Greer.

"I love everything about this," she says, kissing me again.

"Good. Now, let's put this ring on your finger and make it official."

She sits back on her heels and holds her left hand out for me. I slide the ring on just as everyone reaches us on the sand.

"Let me see!" The girls huddle around her as all the guys pat my back or shake my hand.

"It's beautiful."

"Stunning."

"It's so shiny!"

"He did a great job."

"Yeah." Nat looks over at me, and my eyes meet hers. "He did real *nice*."

I let out a throaty laugh and then swoop her into my arms.

"What did I tell you about calling me nice?"

She shrugs playfully in the way she always does.

"I guess you better remind me."

"Oh, I plan to."

And later that night, I did.

Twice.

Already want more from Tobias and Natalie?
Keep reading for a Bonus Epilogue.

BONUS EPILOGUE
NATALIE

Ten years later

I love days without wind—sunshine and warm weather to soothe the soul. I have a drink in one hand as I sit on my back patio in my cushion chair, with the faint sound of music playing around me as I soak it all in.

Life.

Life is good, and it's so real—

"Ahhhh!" The high-pitched squeal of my nine-year-old daughter, Nina, fills my ears as she runs past me. Her twin brother, Dixon, is behind her with a squirt gun. Getting pregnant on the beach trip where Tobias and I got engaged wasn't ideal, but our life has been nothing short of amazing since we jumped all in.

I sit up, lower my sunglasses, and survey the yard.

Another reason I'm enjoying this day is because of all the people who are here right now.

Ten years later, Tobias's annual barbecue is still in full swing. Only now, kids are running around, babies are crawling in the grass, and a TV is hung on the back of the house with the first Saturday night college football game of the season preparing to start.

This is how we have planned the barbecue for the last few years. June is great, but late August is even better because it means we can all get together and watch Simon's son, Grey, playing with his college team.

"I hope summer lasts for at least another month before the cool weather shows up," Greer says, taking the seat next to me and handing me a margarita.

"Me too," Calla says as Willa, Paige, and Nora join us.

The guys are all huddled around the grill.

"Does Zane ever take that off?" I ask, sipping my drink and sighing at how refreshing it is.

"We went through three of them, and this one is his favorite," Willa answers.

All of us turn to look at him and at the baby carrier strapped around his body with their newborn, their third daughter, passed out against his chest.

"That's why Graham bought ours," Paige adds.

I smile at how he looks like Zane; only Paige and Graham's daughter is four months old.

"I'm plugging in the bounce house," Nina says as she runs up to us.

"Okay, be careful with the little ones."

The ages range from newborn to eleven, and in total, there are nine kids.

It's a madhouse, but I wouldn't have it any other way.

"It's back on," Simon shouts, then grabs the remote to turn the TV up.

"There he is!" Greer cheers as Grey takes the field. His

team has the ball first. None of us speak as the ball hits Grey's hands. He takes one step back before sending the football flying through the air. His teammate catches it and sprints down the field.

"Go, go, go!" Simon yells. Tobias, Graham, and Hero join in on the chant.

"Yeah!" We all erupt when Grey's team scores the first touchdown of the game in less than two minutes.

Hugs and high-fives make their way around the group.

I love that we get to share these moments together. I lean back, taking in the group around me. These are my best friends. We have watched each other fall in love, get married, have kids, and become parents, and now we are watching one of those said kids achieve their own goals and dreams. It's absolutely mind-blowing to be part of this life. I wouldn't trade it for the world.

"Dove, can you come help me for a moment?" Tobias says as he walks past me and into the kitchen through the sliding doors.

I set my drink down and follow him. As soon as we are inside, he grabs my hand, tugging me through the house and up the stairs.

"What is happening?" I ask with a smile. For some, that playful side of becoming a new couple fades, but not with Tobias. He's been trying to sneak me off to fool around for years, and I assume this is no different.

"You know we have a full house downstairs, right?"

We reach our office, and he closes the door.

"I know, but I just had an email come through, and I wanted to share it with you alone."

I narrow my gaze at him.

This must be some news. His eyes brighten as he grins at me. All these years and that smile still makes my heart beat a little faster.

"Sit," he says.

I sit at my desk and watch him grab his laptop to join me.

He's beaming with excitement the entire time as he logs in and pulls up this very mysterious email.

Then, he spins the computer for me to see.

I scan it quickly and then suck in a breath, my hands coming to my mouth to cover it.

"No," I whisper. "Is this real?"

I point at the screen as Tobias nods.

"It's very real, Nat. We did it. The entire series, including our release two weeks ago, is a bestseller, and now Hulu wants it—all of it."

My heart leaps as quickly as I do to move around his desk and hug him.

Our first book together was a hit. So we wrote another and another, and before we knew it, we were three series deep. Our latest is a small-town slow-burn series that follows a group of friends. It's my favorite series to date, and I'm beyond thrilled that everyone agrees with me.

"We did it," I whisper.

My next words get lodged in my throat as my eyes begin to water.

Tobias gently grips my chin, forcing me to turn and look him in the eyes.

He doesn't say anything, but he doesn't have to. I feel it, too.

His lips gently touch mine as I wrap my arms around his neck to make this kiss last longer.

Falling for my best friend was the best choice I've ever made.

Want more from Jami?
The Asher Family (set in Lovers) is available now on Amazon and kicks off with the oldest Asher brother, Hudson.

Join Jami's mailing list for exclusive bonus epilogues, giveaways, and all the book news!

Please leave a review for Always Been Write on the retailer where you purchased the book.
Thank you!

MORE BOOKS BY JAMI ROGERS

For the full list of titles by Jami Rogers, please scan the QR below.

FOLLOW JAMI

Want more from Jami?

Join Jami's mailing list for exclusive bonus epilogues, giveaways, and all the book news!

Visit her website
www.authorjamirogers.com

Or join Team Jami Rogers on Instagram
@TeamJamiRogers

facebook.com/AuthorJamiRogers

instagram.com/authorjamirogers

bookbub.com/authors/authorjamirogers

goodreads.com/jamirogers

tiktok.com/@authorjamirogers

ACKNOWLEDGMENTS

I'm always at a loss for words by the time I reach the final book in a series, especially regarding the acknowledgments. How can I thank the team who has been with me through all six books differently than I have before?

Dana Volney, Julie Sturgeon, Hang Le, Jenny Sliger, Jen DeJong, Grant, and Brixon, you have all been the best team I could ever ask for. I say that a lot, but I mean it more and more with each book. I LOVE working with every single one of you. Each of you made me fall more in love with the writing/publishing process because of the fantastic work you produce. I am forever thankful for you.

My ARC team and the ARC readers who have joined me through Grey's Promotions … you are the best! Thank you for taking a chance on me and my stories and for sharing them with the world. You truly make my heart so happy. I am so grateful for all of you.

Cheers to the next series!

ABOUT THE AUTHOR

My name is Jami Rogers and I write fun, fast, and flirty slow-burn contemporary romance novels with heat. I *love* love and want to share my passion for happily ever afters with the world.

I was born in Wyoming and still live in the cowboy state with my husband, daughter, and dog. I like to read, write, run, watch movies/TV, and spend time with my family. I'm horrible at returning phone calls and prefer to text, but I still struggle to hit the little blue arrow to send a message once I'm finished typing my reply. My husband does 90% of the cooking in our house. Not because I'm busy – I'm just simply a lousy cook.

www.authorjamirogers.com

Want more from Jami?
Join Jami's mailing list for exclusive bonus epilogues, giveaways, and all the book news!

facebook.com/AuthorJamiRogers

instagram.com/jami_s_rogers

goodreads.com/jamirogers

bookbub.com/profile/jami-rogers

tiktok.com/@authorjamirogers

www.ingramcontent.com/pod-product-compliance
Lightning Source LLC
Chambersburg PA
CBHW022108310726
48972CB00007B/1939